JOYRIDE

CLASS

CREATED BY
PATRICK NESS

JOYRIDE
GUY ADAMS

BOOKS

1 3 5 7 9 10 8 6 4 2

BBC Books, an imprint of Ebury Publishing
20 Vauxhall Bridge Road,
London SW1V 2SA

BBC Books is part of the Penguin Random House group of companies
whose addresses can be found at global.penguinrandomhouse.com

Penguin
Random House
UK

This book is published to accompany the television series entitled *Class*
first broadcast on BBC Three in 2016. *Class* is a BBC Wales production.

Executive producers: Patrick Ness, Steven Moffat and Brian Minchin

First published by BBC Books in 2016

www.penguin.co.uk

A CIP catalogue record for this book is available from the British Library

ISBN 9781785941863

Printed and bound in Great Britain by Clays Ltd, St Ives PLC

Penguin Random House is committed to a sustainable future for our
business, our readers and our planet. This book is made from Forest
Stewardship Council® certified paper.

MIX
Paper from
responsible sources
FSC
www.fsc.org   FSC® C018179

To my favourite nephew, James.
Who always ensures the cats will be fed.

1

THEY SAY SHOCK DOES STRANGE THINGS

Bizarrely, the first thing out of Poppy's mum's mouth when she hears the news is 'But she hasn't passed her test.' They say shock does strange things.

It's true. Poppy has been saving up for her lessons, working weekends and evenings to get the money together. In fact, in saving up her cash, she showed exactly the sort of single-minded determination that is in full evidence when she punctures the betting shop window with the bonnet of a stolen car. It's the only thing she does that evening that's true to character.

Poppy has always been fastidious. Her friends mock her for the obsessive way she keeps her room tidy, everything in its right place. There's no sign of that as she hangs through the shattered windscreen of the car, bloodied and dusted with crystals of shattered glass, head like a stomped-on jam doughnut. Still, if the confetti of betting slips that twirl around her as she dies upset her, she doesn't show it. She's laughing through a ruptured throat, a wet explosion of humour, spluttering its last across the chrome paintwork of the bonnet long before the ambulance arrives.

Stephen Patrick is still sore from his chosen horse limping its way around Aintree as if it's diseased or suicidal. He *hates* that laugh. It reminds him of childhood nightmares. A creature in his bathroom sink. Gurgled death threats from beyond the U-bend. 'She weren't right in the head,' he tells the investigating police officer.

'No kidding,' thinks WPC Delano as she scribbles down his comments in her notebook.

WPC Delano draws the short straw and is forced to tell Poppy's parents why their daughter won't be coming home. Ever. She sits on their immaculate, floral-patterned sofa in silence while they stare, argue, stare some more and then eventually cry. Throughout all this Delano is barely there, her head replaying the sight of Poppy being pulled back inside the car by the SOCOs, her loose face flapping and squeaking on the car paintwork.

Delano's next job is to trace the full stop of the crash back to wherever the incident started. It isn't difficult. Poppy – mousey Poppy, insecure and nervous Poppy – tore through Shoreditch like a weather front.

Ten minutes before she dies, she's in the middle of her shift behind the 'oven fresh' counter of Morefields, the supermarket where she works. Her skin and hair are oily from the grease of the roast chickens that slow-dance around the rotisserie.

She's never given any sign of hating the job, it is what it is, a way of making money. A short cut to a car and better nights out.

According to the department manager, she simply stops what she's doing, takes off the plastic trilby hat staff are forced to wear, its brim turned slightly yellow from poultry fat, and flings it into the air like a cheap frisbee. She then climbs over the counter itself, feet crushing steak bakes and cheese and onion slices, and walks out of the shop, leaving slowly diminishing, meaty footprints behind her.

The department manager catches up with her at the automatic doors but she ignores his angry questions, shoving him into a display of chocolates and making her way out into the car park.

If anyone suspects this isn't the first time Poppy has stolen a car, the meal she makes of it sets them straight.

After twenty seconds spent trying to break the driver's window of a silver Honda with a small stone and a lot of screaming, she should, by rights, end her sudden streak of rebellion right there. But the woman who rushes over to stop her is holding her own car keys in her hand. Three vicious punches later and Poppy is running towards the open driver's door of her new ride, its owner howling on the ground with a broken nose.

Roar of ignition, crump of metal as she reverses back into the car parked behind her and then a squeal of petrified tyres as she's tearing out of the car park at fifty miles per hour. Behind her, the car she rammed is blaring out its alarm like an indignant old lady, unable to quite believe the sheer audacity of the behaviour she's just witnessed.

It's pure good luck that there's a break in the traffic as Poppy pulls out onto the road. Fortunate too that the solitary pedestrian on the zebra crossing is quick enough to throw herself out of the way before Poppy hits her.

The sluggish traffic is bothering some people, tutting and complaining, offering frequent insults to the traffic lights. It doesn't bother Poppy. Poppy doesn't seem bothered by *anything* as she hammers the horn and straddles the white line, other cars veering out of her way as she refuses to slow down.

One guy, still seething from a particularly lousy meeting at the head office of the marketing company where he works, decides there's no way he's going to be the one to back down. He's spent the last two hours backing down. Gregson, still swaggering from the success of his pitiful campaign for a broadband supplier, had trashed every single one of his ideas until, by the end of the meeting, the oily little sod had won the damn account off him. No more. This silly cow coming up on him was going to have to be the one to swerve. He's thinking that right up until he yanks the steering wheel at the last minute and sends his car into the back of a truck delivering building supplies. The second to last thing that goes through his head is 'Why does today hate me so much?' The last thing to go through his head is a piece of scaffolding. His lousy day ends with his head looking like an angry cocktail cherry.

If Poppy notices she doesn't care. She's now four minutes away from the window of the betting shop and a final, brief leap through the windscreen of this car.

Nobody calls the police, they're far too busy filming Poppy on their phones. The news channels are spoilt for choice when it comes to wobbly camera footage. That evening Poppy will be a TV star, or at least the back of her head will be. There is only one, vaguely useable shot of her from the front and it shows a face that even her closest friends don't recognise: a wild, screaming, laughing, evil face, all teeth and eyes so big they look like they're about to bounce down onto her red cheeks.

The last casualty of the journey – other than herself – is a man trying to fit a stepladder into the backseat of his car. It's not Poppy that hits him, it's a car veering out of her way, slamming the back door on him so hard you could have folded his remains like a shop display T-shirt.

Two minutes away from the betting shop window.

A group of school kids cheer as Poppy goes past. To them this seems fun, a bit of action to break up the long trudge home. Something they can message their mates about later. They won't let facts get in the way of a good story, each of them will claim they were nearly hit by the car, each of them will claim they heard her laughing as she went by (she *was* laughing by all accounts, laughing every minute of the way but there's no way they could have heard it over the roar of the engine and the constant beeping of car horns). One of them will even insist they got off with Poppy at a party, as if breathlessly cupping the breast of someone who would later go on to kill herself confers magic onto them.

One minute away from the betting shop window.

The last race at Aintree has been run. Nobody's made their fortunes. Stephen Patrick tears up his betting slip, takes a sip of cold, vending machine tea and wonders whether he can be bothered to cook tonight. Maybe he'll just stop in at the chippy on the way home. Oh, and, by the way, what's all the noise outside? Car horns and a revving engine. Sounds like some kind of carnival is heading his way.

When the window breaks it sounds as if someone has let a firecracker off in the shop. The air is full of noise and glass. Nobody screams or shouts, it's all too sudden for that, there's just a lot of confused spinning and stumbling. Seconds ago, most people in the room were cursing their bad luck. Five minutes later and they'll have changed their minds. It's frankly phenomenal that nobody is seriously hurt. This isn't a big shop, in fact on major race days regular customers complain about the fact – but then they complain about most things – it certainly isn't big enough that you should be able to drive a car through it without killing everyone. There are injuries of course, you don't add a rainstorm of shattered glass to a room without drawing a little blood. One of the older customers dislocates his hip as he's knocked back against the wall.

Strangely, the worst injured of all is Mandy Taylor who's working behind the counter. She's so shocked to see a car driving towards her inside her place of work, a building not commonly troubled by motor traffic, that she topples back off her stool and cracks her head open on the low shelf behind her. She'll have serious concussion and a neck injury that will flare up for years to come.

'Why do you think she did it?' WPD Delano's partner asks her as they lie in bed that night. The police officer's head is still replaying the sight of Poppy as her dead body is pulled back inside the darkness of the car. It's like prey being pulled back into a bear's cave, she thinks, battered and beaten, softened up for easy chewing.

'I haven't a clue,' she tells him. 'Not the first idea.'

She's not alone.

2

A PRETEND NAME FOR
A PRETEND HUMAN

'It doesn't make sense. If I kick it to death will it start to make sense?'

'Madame?'

Quill turns from the Oyster top-up machine and stares George Barker in the eye. He decides he'd fancy her if she wasn't so terrifying. Then he decides he fancies her anyway and worries quite what that says about him.

'You work here?'

'I don't wear the uniform for fun, madame.'

'That's not entirely my experience of uniforms.'

'Oh aye?' He attempts a cheeky smile. He *thinks* it's a cheeky smile, without a mirror to hand it's hard to tell. Cheeky smiles are not something he gets a lot of practice at. By the way her expression somehow manages to get even *more* hostile he guesses he may have been slightly off the mark. Either that or she is entirely immune to cheeky smiles.

'No,' she says, 'don't get that look on your face you awful, awful man.'

He tries to turn the smile that may have been, but most probably wasn't, cheeky into a look of genuine concern and sympathy. He's not bad at that look. When you work for London Transport you tend to use it quite often. In fact, it's probably his second most well-worn look, narrowly beaten by 'firm but polite refusal'.

'What look, madame?'

'The look that suggests you're imagining something sordid regarding uniforms. If I see it again I'm likely to punch you.'

'We have a firm policy with regard abuse of staff, madame.'

'I bet you do, you'd have to, working in this hellhole. You're probably fending off justifiable assassination attempts on the hour, every hour.' The woman relaxes slightly. 'This stupid machine won't top up my Oyster Card.'

'I see, let me have a look.'

He moves to the machine and starts tapping away at the touchscreen in the sort of manner he hopes conveys extreme professionalism, the sort of manner that broadcasts his ability to Get Things Done. She just stares at the crowds around them with a slight look of disgust.

'Look at them,' she says, 'they don't have a problem. They're all about their soya milk lattes and their copies of the *Metro*. I've led armies, fought wars, I have held dying comrades in my arms and fought on.'

'Oh yes?' he says, not really listening because the machine is misbehaving and trying to offer him a return to Basildon.

'And now I can't even get a few stops on the Central line without it all being a drama.'

'I know what you mean,' he mumbles, wondering why he's now looking at a five-day pass. 'I'm not sure the machine's working properly.'

'I told you that didn't I?'

'Yes, madame, I suppose you did. If you come to the counter, I'll top it up there.'

'Joy.'

The woman with too many names, none of which feel quite like her own any more, walks into the corner shop, having finally managed to top up her card and get home.

'Hello Miss Quill,' someone says as they walk past her and out of the door.

'Who the hell was that?' she wonders. They sounded infuriatingly cheerful. She's half a mind to give chase and push them into a puddle just to teach them a lesson about life. Lesson. Yes. It was Danielle Westby, year eleven. She has tried to teach her physics. Tried to teach her physics in the same way one might try to teach a dog how to repair the engine on a light aircraft.

Miss Quill. A pretend name for a pretend human. How tedious it all is.

Once, light years from here, she had been a rebel leader, fighting the Rhodia, willing to die for freedom (or, at the very least, the pleasure of really bloodying their supercilious noses). Then she had been captured and forced into the slavery of the young Rhodian prince. They put a creature in her brain, a tiny, single-minded thing of teeth and claws. The creature will kill her unless she protects the prince. It will also kill her if she uses any weapon other than her own hands. Basically, it takes all the fun out of life and gives her the odd migraine into the bargain. Joy.

The great rebel is now bonded to the will of her enemy. Well, the only one left alive, because shortly after her capture, the Shadow Kin wiped both her and the prince's people out and forced the two of them into hiding. The scourge of the Rhodia, now disguised and trapped on a backwater planet being forced to teach dumb children and, even worse, do grocery shopping.

She walks along the shop aisles, staring at strange food she loathes the taste of and can't really be bothered to buy. In the old days she would simply have raided this entire building for necessary supplies, leaving a trail of blood and destruction. That was an honest way of gathering food and supplies, nobody would ask you for a store loyalty card or try to indulge in small talk. How she misses it.

Eventually, she throws a few tins of baked beans into a hand basket just to show that she can adapt to anything given time, even shopping. Deciding to really go for broke she adds a sliced brown loaf, along with something that rattles in its pack like the desiccated remains of a corpse (glancing at the label it will apparently become edible if she pours boiling water on it) and a box of breakfast cereal that manages to look healthy and yet also insufferably smug and childish at the same time. She stares at the box for a minute, hating the appalling beautiful people who are skipping along a beach while the wind makes their hair flow out behind them like banners of war. She drops the box in her basket and decides that that's quite enough shopping for today.

'Hello,' says the man behind the counter. 'Would you like a bag?'

'Absolutely, with the way today's been going, I can suffocate myself with it later.'

He looks confused for a moment. 'They put little holes in them now,' he says eventually, 'so you can't.'

'Spoilsports.'

She asks for a small bottle of vodka as well, because this amount of being dull and human demands a reward.

Shopping safely stowed away in her non-lethal carrier bag, she walks home, hoping with every step that the house will be empty when she gets there.

It isn't. The front room is infested with annoying young people. She wonders if that awful shop will sell her a spray to deal with them.

One is the young man who is as much 'Charlie' as she is 'Miss Quill'. He is the enslaver, ruler of a toppled people, prince of a dead world and infrequent tidier of his room. The other is his insufferably pretty boyfriend Matteusz. He is Polish, which, as far as Quill can tell means he's human but uses slightly less conjunctions.

'Have you seen this?' Charlie is waving an iPad at her. Naturally her first instinct is to take it off him and slap him silly with it, but that's not allowed. The creature in her brain wasn't put there specifically to stop her hitting people with iPads but she has no doubt it features on the long list of 'No, You Can't Do That'.

She walks past him, ignoring the question and heads straight into the kitchen. Maybe she can just crawl into one of the kitchen cupboards with her bag of shopping, spend a quiet evening in with a loaf of bread and a bottle of vodka. Never let it be said she has no class, she'll even use a saucepan to drink out of rather than just neck it straight from the bottle.

'I said, Have you seen this?' Charlie has followed her. Of course he has. She glances at the iPad and sees a news item about some girl who has stolen a car and driven it into a shop window.

'No, should I have?' She starts unpacking the shopping, anything to distract her from his silly, open, naive little face.

'It's very strange.'

'So are skinny jeans, doesn't mean I want to spend my time thinking about them.'

'She stole a car.'

'I can see that, so what?'

'It just wasn't like her. Then she drove it into a shop.'

Quill wishes she'd bought more things, she's now trapped in a dull conversation with nothing to save her but an empty carrier bag. Maybe she'll put it over her head after all, hide away in a cosy blue and white hood until everyone has gone away.

'You knew her?' she asks.

'No, but April did. She said she was nice.'

'April says *everyone's* nice. It's her disease.'

'Fine,' Charlie knows better than to keep trying. 'Matteusz is staying.'

'Of course he is, good job I bought two tins of beautiful, luxurious baked beans then.'

'Is that all we've got?'

'The shop is just down the road, feel free to use it.'

Charlie sighs and walks back into the other room. Quill relaxes a little. No doubt he and Matteusz will now be sharing looks of teenage suffering with one another. It could be worse, at least they do that quietly.

What does it matter that some girl has stolen a car and lost control of it? Is it any wonder in this crushing, stupid, insipid little world? The girl probably looked out of her window one morning and felt the horrid banality of it all, decided to do something – anything – to escape it.

'Suicide?' says a little voice in her head. 'You think that's a worthy way out of a life that's suffocating you?' No. She doesn't. Of course she doesn't. That's why she's still here, living in a hell ruled by an irritating man-child. Death isn't a problem, she's chased that often enough, but it's a gift you're given by other people.

She looks at her watch. It's six o'clock. How is she supposed to fill the hours between now and unconsciousness? She picks up one of the tins. With beans? Will they make existence better? Probably not.

In the other room she can hear her jailer and Matteusz talking. It's alright for him isn't it? He gathers people to him like flies. Their whole world is gone, trapping them in a universe that may as well be empty. But not for him. He has new people. He's made friends. She has nothing, her closest companion is the thing in her brain that is invisible right up until the point it kills her. What a lucky woman she is. To have fought her whole life for this. It wasn't the deal. She gave her life to the cause, she would either win justice for her people or she would die trying. This? Who said *this* was something she should have to bear?

She toasts some bread, pours beans on them – cold, because she's now so desperate to get away from the noise of Charlie and Matteusz next door that the idea of waiting even a few minutes longer is unbearable – and takes them upstairs to her room.

As she walks past they go silent for a moment. They've been talking about her. Great. Whatever. Miserable Quill. Unreasonable Quill. Angry Quill. All true. Deal with it.

She eats her cold beans as if they've done something to offend her.

17

* * *

A few hours pass and the evening refuses to just end. She sits in her room and stares at the wall. She tried watching TV for a bit, but it angered her more than the silence. What were soaps for? Were these human's lives so empty of incident they had to absorb fictional ones? Someone had been shouting about a baby. Someone else had been having an affair. A third person was stealing money from the company at which he worked. All of it delivered with the sort of screaming banality that humans liked to think made something seem real. At no point did anyone shoot anyone else. The angry young woman working behind the bar in the local pub didn't take the small knife she used for cutting slices of lemon and plunge it into the eye of the loud idiot who was sexually harassing her. Quill wonders how this species has ever got anything done. How are they still alive? *How dare they be still alive?* It isn't fair. Absolutely nothing is even slightly fair.

She turns off the lights in her room, making do with the second-hand glow of the streetlights outside. She remembers another world, a world of violent skies and hot sands. A world she had thrived in, right up until it had burned.

Eventually she falls asleep and dreams of being someone else.

3

BE READY FOR THE TIME
OF YOUR LIFE

'It's a thrill, yeah?'

'Of course it is. The biggest. The best.'

'Should be, the amount I'm paying.'

'It's worth every penny.'

'And safe? You sure it's safe?'

'I wouldn't be selling it otherwise, I'd hardly stay in business without repeat custom. This isn't something I advertise remember?'

'No, suppose not.'

'This isn't something you run an advert for in the paper. A glossy flyer through a letterbox. All of my clients come to me via the recommendation of someone on my current list. No strangers. You're all vetted. I don't believe in unnecessary risks.'

'Vetted?'

'That's right.'

'So you've looked into me, yeah?'

'Of course.'

'And what did you find about me?'

'Everything. But most importantly the two things that I really needed to know.'

'Which were?'

'You've got money and you keep your mouth shut.'

'Ha! Yeah, that's fair enough.'

'Because you know the penalty don't you?'

'Penalty?'

'For talking about this. This isn't something you share with your mates down the pub, or in the office come the morning. This isn't something you brag about.'

'I know that. Like you said, I can keep my mouth shut.'

'Good, because if you don't – and don't give me that look, I say this to everybody, seriously, absolutely *everybody* – someone will find you.'

'Ha!'

'No, don't laugh, I mean it. Someone will find you and you won't see it coming. You won't recognise them, you won't know them. But they will know you. And they'll kill you.'

'Look… I'm not paying all this money to be threatened, yeah?'

'No, you're paying all this money to have the most amazing experience you can dream of. You're paying this money for something incredible. For an experience unlike anything else. And you know what else?'

'What?'

'After tonight you'll be begging me to take your money all over again. You won't be able to wait. So, you're ready?'

'Course I am!'

'Then lie back, relax and be ready for the time of your life.'

4

SOMETIMES A BED CAN BECOME EMPTY (EVEN WHEN THERE'S SOMEONE IN IT)

Sex changes a bed. Before it happens it's a place of potential, afterwards it can be a number of things. Sometimes it's warm, comforting, the best place in the world. Sometimes it's cold, awkward, a place you're waiting to leap out of, desperate for the moment that doing so won't make you seem awful. Sometimes, thinks Matteusz, it becomes empty, even when there's still a Charlie in it.

Charlie's staring up at the ceiling but his eyes are working in reverse. He's looking inside, he's lost in his own head. This is not the first time. Matteusz is used to self-absorbed. He's known a lot of self-absorbed. Charlie is different. Matteusz sometimes thinks Charlie's head contains more than he'll ever be able to imagine.

'You are thinking about the girl,' Matteusz says. 'The dead one.'

It takes a minute for Charlie to come back into the room, to hear the words and answer. 'Yes.'

'Why?'

Charlie turns to look at him. 'Why?'

'Yes. I have to ask that now. Our lives are not the same any more. A few weeks ago we would hear about something awful, something strange, and we would think about it as...' Matteusz thinks about this, about how to express it, 'as something far away. Sad but not part of our life. We'd feel bad about it. Talk about it. Maybe even donate money to someone on JustGiving to help make an awful thing seem better. Now, everything horrible seems to be part of our lives. Something that we will end up living. Are you thinking about the girl as a sad thing that is far away or are you wondering if it is part of our lives?'

'It's hard to tell, isn't it?'

'See? That's what I mean. Our lives have changed. You can't think that everything bad that happens is something to do with us. If you do you will be miserable forever.'

Charlie frowns. 'But it is strange, isn't it? It wasn't like her. Why would she do it?'

'You think someone made her?' Matteusz sits up, pushing the pillows behind him.

'Maybe. I don't know.'

'Or maybe she broke, something inside her just…' Matteusz doesn't finish, simply sighs. 'You know what I think?'

Charlie rolls onto his front, looking up at Matteusz. 'No, what?'

'I think you are too used to being a prince.'

Charlie smiles. 'I've never been anything else.'

'And that is the problem. You are not a prince here, you are not responsible for all of your people. You are just Charlie.'

'Just?'

Matteusz smiles. 'OK, not 'just' to me but you know what I mean. You have a problem with responsibility.'

'I don't think I do. I've been responsible for people all of my life.'

'*That's* the problem you have. Now, here, people will do whatever they want and it's nothing to do with you.'

'I'm supposed not to care?'

'Of course you care, only a horrible person does not care, but you're not supposed to think it's a problem you have to solve. We're not all your subjects. We're not all your responsibility.'

Charlie stares at him for a moment then rolls onto his back. Why are they even having this conversation?

'You think I don't know that?' he says. 'I don't have any subjects any more, do I? I don't have any people.'

'No, you just have friends, and friends are *better* than subjects because subjects have no choice. They're born to love you.'

Charlie opens his mouth to speak but, try as he might, he can't untangle everything he's feeling. It feels like he's being caressed and slapped, all at the same time.

'Nobody was born to love me. My world wasn't about love. Not like that. Not in the way you mean. But it's difficult, isn't it? Ever since what happened… ever since…'

'The prom.' Just thinking about it makes Matteusz feel cold. He pulls the sheet up around him.

'Yes. There always seems to be something waiting to hurt us. To attack us. Kill us.'

'She stole a car and drove it into a shop,' Matteusz says. 'That's not alien. There were no monsters, no weird…' he waves his hand in the air, 'monster things, space things, hole in the universe things… This was just a girl who did something terrible. It is not good. It is sad. But it isn't something we have to feel the weight of.'

'But how do we know that? He told us…'

'The man from space, the man who saved you and Miss Quill?'

'Yes.'

Matteusz can see that Charlie is thinking about the man. The impossible man. The Doctor. 'He told us we would have to be careful. He told us we would have to help protect people, to fight. Talk about responsibility. It's not about being a prince, it's about him. It's about what we promised.'

'But that doesn't mean that everything that happens is *about* that, that's all I'm saying.'

'I know.' Charlie moves up the bed and slips under the sheet, lying back on Matteusz's chest. 'I just don't know how you're supposed to tell. There was a thing on the news the other day, a woman who ran through a supermarket naked, then dived into one of the freezers.'

'Maybe she was excited by their special offers.'

Charlie smiles. 'But I sat there wondering if she was possessed. Or running away from some kind of…' His voice tapers off and Matteusz knows he is thinking of the Shadow Kin, of how they made Charlie run, run all the way to another world.

'Evil alien?'

'We're all aliens somewhere,' Charlie says.

His phone beeps with a message alert. Charlie reaches over to the bedside table, picks it up and reads the message.

'What is it?' asks Matteusz.

'Tanya,' says Charlie, showing him the phone. 'Something else has happened.'

27

5

DESIGNED TO MAKE NORMAL HUMANS CRY

Thick jungle. Buzz of insects. In the distance a bird calls out before exploding up through the canopy and into the world of daylight outside. Keeping low, Tanya pushes through the foliage. She knows the rebels are here, knows it even before she hears them moving through their camp.

She hangs back, watching for a moment, getting a read on how many people are there. One of them is gutting a pig while another prepares a fire on which to cook it. A few feet away, the leader and his lieutenant are squatting on the ground, conferring over a map. Their rifles are on the ground next to them, but that shouldn't make her cocky, they'll be aiming and firing in seconds if she lets them. A fifth man works on one of the tents, tugging at a canvas they've stretched between the low branches of the trees. His rifle is on his back.

This is an opportunity. They're relaxed, not expecting trouble.

She bursts through the treeline, automatic weapon bucking and coughing in her arms as she shoots. She takes the leader and his lieutenant first, map blown to confetti that showers over their flailing bodies. Then the man preparing the fire, then his butcher friend who ends up looking as much like dinner as the pig by the time she's done. Finally, the man fixing the tent. He's had the chance to pull the rifle from his back but not the time to aim it. Tanya takes him down with two bursts.

There is silence, then a crack of automatic pistol fire. She hears herself grunt as she's hit. It's only a flesh wound, she can deal with it. A man she hadn't accounted for is running towards her through the trees. She drops to one knee and fires upward. His head opens like a blossoming jungle flower. A Jackson Pollock-splatter on the tent behind him, then he hits the ground.

Tanya has taken the camp. She celebrates with a Mars Bar.

'Damn girl,' says her brother, Jarvis, 'you scare me.'

Tanya hands him the controller. 'You take over, I've got homework.'

'Why bother? You were born to be a marine.'

'Nah… the uniform's too dull.'

She heads upstairs, the sound of the digital jungle returning then fading behind her as Jarvis continues the mission to rid the world of all evil pixels.

For a while she's lost in the world of numbers, not only the work she has to do but – and she would never admit this to anyone at school because she struggles making friends as it is – a few bigger calculations that occur to her during her working. Sometimes it's just nice to solve the puzzle. Numbers do as they're told, they always make sense. They'll always find order if you poke them the right way. Tanya sometimes wishes she could solve people so easily. People just never quite add up.

Then, because she's on a roll, she pokes at her physics homework. Naturally, it's designed to make normal humans cry, because Miss Quill set it. If Miss Quill were able to fold mouserabbittraps or sprinkle anthrax bacteria into the pages of her student's text books, Tanya thinks she'd probably do it, if only to break up a boring afternoon.

After half an hour or so of calculating centripetal force she rewards herself by falling down the rabbit hole of the internet, strolling from one link to another.

She checks out Seraphin videos for a few minutes, then when she is bored of his hair (no, not bored, you could no more get bored of Seraphin's hair than you could eating ice cream, she is simply, temporarily full) she moves on.

From there it's a spiral of one Buzzfeed list after another: top ten cute goats, the fourteen best autocorrect mistakes, 'You won't believe what happens to this puppy, I laughed and cried!'

Finally, scrolling through her Facebook timeline, she sees the news that will ruin her night. Because there's no way Max Collins could have done that, right? Not Max. Max was a nice guy. Max was together. Max was normal.

Tanya reads, feels her guts churn, then messages her friends.

6

MAX WAS A NICE GUY

Tommy Collins is used to hearing his big brother wandering around at night. Max always stays up late, playing his Xbox with his headphones on. Tommy hates it, not because it disturbs him but because Max gets away with it. Never are the nine years between them felt more keenly than in those faint creaks of the floorboards in the early hours of the morning. Sure, Max sometimes gets a vague word of warning from Mum or Dad, a little comment thrown away over the breakfast table with no more weight than the passing of marmalade. 'Of course, if you didn't stay up so late you wouldn't be so tired,' or 'I suppose you were up to all hours again, you've got bags beneath your eyes the size of suitcases.' That last one was always delivered with a chuckle, as if it were the funniest joke in the world. Tommy hadn't thought it was funny the first time let alone the hundredth.

One of the biggest worries Tommy has about getting old is the fact that he might be stuck using the same expressions for everything all the time: 'Raining cats and dogs again.' 'I'm so tired I could sleep for England.' 'Cheer up, it could be serious.' Tommy watches his parents sometimes, staring into space, staring at the telly, staring out the window, and he wonders how miserable being old must be.

But not so miserable he doesn't want to get on with it, because then he'll be allowed to stay up as late as Max.

Tonight, Tommy decides he'll follow Max downstairs. Not because he's hungry or thirsty, just because he can. As if it might prove something.

He gets out of bed and moves as quietly as he can to his bedroom door, turning the handle gently and stepping out onto the upstairs landing. In his parents' room he can hear his dad snoring. ('Like a train coming into the station.')

Downstairs, Max sounds like he's unlocking the internal door that leads to the garage. What does he want out there at this time of night? There's nothing in there but tools and junk. Midnight snack, glass of juice, that's normal enough, but is Max planning on mowing the lawn by moonlight? The weirdness of it makes Tommy even more angry.

He goes downstairs, paying extra attention to the fourth step from the bottom because he knows it creaks.

Once he's in the hallway he's not so worried about being careful, as if downstairs is a world away, somewhere you can't possibly hear if you're lying in his parents' bed. He walks into the kitchen to see the door to the garage *is* open. Max is inside, rummaging around.

'What are you doing?' Tommy asks, stepping out into the garage. The dusty concrete floor makes him wish he'd put shoes on.

Max is shocked. 'You made me jump out of my skin! You should be in bed,' he says, which makes Tommy even angrier. It's bad enough when his parents tell him he can't be awake at this time of night, now he has to take it from his brother too? Besides, he hasn't answered the question.

'Well I'm not,' he says, folding his arms then wishing he hadn't, because he knows it makes him look like his mother when she's in a disapproving mood. 'So what are you doing?'

Max stares at him for a few seconds and there's this weird feeling that this isn't his brother he's talking to. It looks like him, sounds like him, but there's something off, something in the way he's standing, something in the way his face twitches as he looks at him. Then Max speaks again and the thought's gone.

'I've had a brilliant idea,' he says, 'want to see?'

Enthusiasm sweeps some of Tommy's anger away. Max is grinning at him and that doesn't happen often. Older brothers just don't grin at their younger brothers, not unless they're about to do something really, really horrible.

'Sure,' says Tommy, unfolding his arms and trying to look grown-up, which is really hard in Iron Man pyjamas.

'Cool,' says Max, 'excellent in fact. Go in the kitchen for a minute, I'll be right with you.'

If Tommy thinks Max's choice of words is weird, another sign that this isn't quite his brother, the thought doesn't hang around. He's gone from angry to eager-to-please with the sort of speed only found in an eight-year-old.

'Pull one of the kitchen chairs out,' Max says as he's leaving, 'put it in the middle of the floor.'

Which is a weird thing to ask him to do, but weird is interesting and Tommy does it. At the last minute, he thinks to lift the chair rather than drag it as he usually would. Downstairs may be a world away from his parents' bedroom but now something genuinely interesting is happening and he's even more determined not to wake them up. He wants to know what Max's plan is.

His brother – or whoever it is that looks like his brother – doesn't keep him waiting, he walks in carrying the large canvas bag his dad uses for his gardening stuff.

'What do you want that for?' Tommy asks.

'Shush,' says Max, 'keep your voice down, we don't want to wake them up do we? Where's the fun in that?'

Tommy nods.

'Sit down in the chair,' Max says, 'this is going to seem weird but you trust me, don't you?'

Tommy nods again. He may not always like Max very much but he does love him and he does trust him. He's mean sometimes but never *really* mean, never properly mean.

'I need to fix you to the chair a bit,' Max says, 'because when I do this I need you to be safe, I need you not to fall off.'

This sounds properly weird now, but still really interesting.

'I won't fall off,' Tommy whispers.

'You say that now, kid,' Max replies, 'but you haven't seen what we're going to do. This is seriously amazing but I don't want you to get accidentally hurt, so just go with me on this, OK?'

Tommy thinks about it.

'I mean,' says Max, 'if you're too scared then…' he shrugs, jostling the bag of gardening tools. There's a rattle of secateurs and trowels.

'Course I'm not scared,' says Tommy, 'it just sounds weird.'

'I guess it does,' says Max, but he knows he's convinced Tommy, and he opens the bag of gardening equipment. 'It *is* pretty weird actually, but in a good way. Put your hands behind your back.'

He pulls out a packet of plastic ties and fixes Tommy's wrists to the bars at the back of the chair. It hurts, and if it were anyone but Max doing it, Tommy would kick off about it. But he doesn't want to look weak in front of his brother, so he doesn't make a noise, not even when Max takes two more ties and straps his ankles to the chair legs.

'I'm not sure about this,' Tommy says without even thinking. If he *had* been thinking he wouldn't have said it, again, not wanting to look scared. But it's true, he *isn't* sure about this. It's weird and not in the good way that Max has said it is.

'Shush,' says Max, 'you've got to be quiet, remember? Really quiet.'

And then, before Tommy can make a noise, Max has slapped some thick tape across his mouth, winding the roll round and round his head. The tape is so tight, Tommy couldn't make a sound now if he tried. He tries to shake the chair, not caring if he wakes his parents up any more, *wanting* to wake them up in fact. Max grabs his face and holds a pair of secateurs up in front of his eyes.

'Sit still you little sod, or I swear I will cut you, understand?'

Tommy looks into his brother's eyes and again he has that feeling that this isn't his brother he's looking at. He's never been scared of his brother, but he's scared now, really scared.

'I mean it,' says Max, 'I will cut pieces off you. I will take your ears off and laugh while I'm doing it.'

Max undoes the little safety clip on the secateurs, opening and closing them with a soft clicking sound.

'Do you believe me?'

Tommy does. That's the awful thing. He really does.

He nods.

'Good. So stay still and stay quiet. Yes?'

Tommy nods again. And he does stay quiet, even during the times Max is out of the room, fetching stuff from the garage, wandering around the house, splashing stuff on the walls, the curtains, the carpet, the sofa. Tommy is particularly worried about what he's splashing on the sofa. He was told off the other day for getting a chocolate thumbprint on the arm, because the sofa was expensive and Mum and Dad are still paying for it in monthly instalments. 'We still don't even really own it,' his mum had said, 'try and wait until it's ours before you ruin it.'

It stinks in the house now, stinks of that stuff Max was throwing around.

Tommy watches as Max gets another chair from the kitchen table and uses it to climb up and open the smoke alarm in the hallway. He takes the plastic covering off and removes the battery inside. 'What does he need a battery for?' Tommy wonders. Max puts the battery in his pocket and then comes back into the kitchen, opens one of the cupboards and pulls out the large metal tin his parents use to keep the good biscuits, the ones in wrappers, the chocolate ones. *Now* he's having a midnight snack,' Tommy thinks, 'after all this? *Now* he's being normal?'

Tommy has a perfect view, through the open door of the kitchen and along the hallway, of Max putting the biscuit tin under his arm and stepping out through the front door. 'OK,' he thinks, 'now you can make noise.' But he doesn't, not yet, because that front door could open again at any minute. Maybe Max is stood right outside it, waiting for an excuse to hurt him.

Max *is* stood right outside and Tommy is relieved when he sees the plastic flap of the letterbox lift up on the front door. 'He was right there all along, waiting to see what I did.'

Then there is the scratch of a match being lit and the small flame drops through the open letterbox and lands on the wet carpet below. There is a heavy, whipping sound, like a rug being shaken and all of a sudden the hallway is on fire. Not just the hallway, the flames are moving along the wet carpet, running into the lounge, creeping up the first few stairs, just as far as the one that creaks.

Now Tommy makes noise, rattling his chair backwards and forwards, backwards and forwards. Hopping it up and down, even though the plastic ties cut into his skin. It doesn't matter, it would take more than this to be heard. Even when his parents realise what's going on and start screaming and shouting, they sound faint against the roaring sound of the flames.

Outside Max – or the thing that looks like Max – sits down on the front lawn, opens the biscuit tin and gets stuck in. He eats one after another, chocolate smearing his smiling lips, as he watches the house go up along with everyone inside it.

7

TWO OF THE THREE OF THEM GOT TO WALK AWAY FROM IT

'Oh God, I burned it…'

April MacLean stares at the charred dustbin lid of a Hawaiian pizza and wants to cry. But that's the last thing her mum needs right now so she'll do what she always does: pretend everything is OK. She can do that, she's always able to do that, it's her superpower. Besides, she won't be crying over the pizza, not really, so why give the charcoal git the satisfaction?

'You alright, love?' her mum shouts from the lounge.

April sighs, takes the pizza and drops it onto the sideboard. It clatters, like a wooden breadboard with bits of pineapple embedded in it. 'Just burned the pizza a bit,' she replies.

She hears the sound of her mum's wheelchair approaching and starts trying to cut the pizza into slices, to go about the business of Everything's Alright.

'I thought I smelled something,' her mum says. 'Sorry, I should have checked it.'

'Don't be silly, it's my fault, I was...' *What* was she? Trapped in her own head that's what. 'Miles away.'

'Is it about the girl in the paper? You knew her didn't you?'

Poppy, yes. That was part of it. But not all, let's be honest, it was just one more thing on top of everything else. One final knife wound in this crazy life.

'A little,' she says, 'she took violin lessons for a while.'

'So sad.'

'Yeah.' Sad. Was that a big enough word? April had run out of words that felt big enough for anything these days. When you shared your heart with a terrifying alien king did you ever really feel something as small as 'sad' any more?

'What makes someone do something like that do you think? Was she...?' Her Mum is now sidling around the notion of drugs, not quite sure if suggesting them is disrespectful.

April puts her out of her misery. 'On something? Don't think so. In fact, no, I know she wasn't, she just wasn't the sort. Poppy was very…' Quiet. Sweet. Nice. Lonely. Very like me. 'She didn't do that kind of thing.'

Her mum nods. 'I hate to think what her parents must be feeling.' Her mum goes quiet and April knows what she's remembering. Because the idea of dying in an out-of-control car is just too close to home isn't it? They're both avoiding that, neither of them wanting the conversation to go there, but that's what they're both thinking. When Poppy crashed her car she killed herself, when her dad crashed his – intentionally, just like Poppy, only with his wife and child onboard – two of three of them got to walk away from it. They were all wounded of course, crippled in different ways, but at least the three of them survived. Just like this pizza – broken but refusing to give up, April thinks, racking up knife-sharp slices on her plate.

'I need to get on with some homework,' she tells her mum. It's a lie and they both know it, but it's by far the easiest way out of this conversation and, for once, her mum lets her take it.

'OK love,' she looks at the pizza and sees something she can fix. 'You sure you don't want me to cook another one for you? That looks… not good.'

'It'll be fine,' April says, biting off a brittle corner as if to prove it. She finds a piece of pineapple in amongst the burned bread and cheese, like a crushed victim buried in the rubble of an earthquake.

Upstairs she finds a message from Tanya and a link to a Facebook post. She reads about Max Collins and finds she just can't eat her pizza any more.

8

TANYA: What's happening? First Poppy and now Max. It's not right.

RAM: furled up.

APRIL: ????

RAM: furling AC.

RAM: FURLING.

RAM: Furl it.

RAM: FURL.

TANYA: Shut up now Ram.

CHARLIE: But what is it? Something must be doing this.

RAM: alien obvs

APRIL: Yeah but how?

TANYA: AND WHY? It's sick. Why would anyone WANT to do it?

CHARLIE: Don't know.

RAM: Cos sick that's why.

CHARLIE: Burning people to death? That's not just sick, that's...

RAM: REALLY SICK.

TANYA: We should get together.

CHARLIE: Yes. Mine?

APRIL: Not now, can't come out now.

TANYA: Neither can I.

APRIL: Talk tomorrow?

9

JUST TRYING

Yeah, thinks Ram, let's talk tomorrow, because talking's great. Talking's the best.

There's been a lot of talking since the prom. He's done his best to avoid most of it. Which mean's there's now been a lot of talking about why he doesn't want to talk.

Ram just wishes that, for once, everyone would be quiet. The inside of his head is filled to bursting with what happened to Rachel. The last thing he wants is to be surrounded by conversations about it. He wants peace from it all. Yes, my girlfriend is dead, killed by Corakinus, King of the Weird Shadow Alien Things who also, by the way, found the time to chop my leg off. Why yes, this new prosthetic limb is alien, how clever of you to notice …

It was difficult enough living through that night, and the scars it left behind, why would he want to talk about it over and over and over again?

Then there was Coach Dawson, more dead, more blood, more screaming. Now this. Poppy and Max... I mean, how many dead bodies is a guy supposed to deal with, you know? This is Shoreditch, the new war zone of the world.

He lies back on his bed and finds all the new places his body aches. Not only is adapting to a new prosthetic tiring and confusing, it makes you hurt in all the wrong places. He's twisting wrong, shifting his balance, favouring this alien mass below his knee. Now he's tearing ligaments, pulling muscles and generally beating himself up without even trying. It wouldn't be so bad if he were actually getting the hang of it. For all his effort, he's playing football like he was only shown a ball a week ago.

'At least you're able to try,' says a voice in his head, 'there's no prosthetic for what happened to Rachel.'

Which is obviously true, but he's still pissed off that the thought bothered to point it out. See? This is the problem with talking, it encourages you to argue with yourself.

He gets up and heads downstairs, because that way at least he can find someone else to argue with.

'You finished your homework?' asks his dad, not even looking up from his magazine.

'See?' thinks Ram. 'And I'm still on the stairs.'

'Just getting a drink,' he says. 'I haven't got much tonight, anyway.'

Varun nods. 'Just checking, I feel like I have to at the moment.'

'No you don't,' Ram replies, already wishing he'd just stayed in his room. 'I even managed to tie my own shoelaces this morning.'

He heads into the kitchen and pours himself a glass of water. Now he has to decide whether it would be easier to stand there and drink it or walk back through and try and get up the stairs before his dad says something else annoying. His dad, however, is only too happy to throw a surprise tackle in.

'What's this I see in the paper about that girl?' he shouts through from the front room. 'Stole a car and killed herself in it.'

'Didn't know her,' says Ram, having decided to take the water and move quickly with it, aiming for the goal of the stairs.

Another tackle, just as he has one foot on the first step.

'I'm trying my best you know,' says his dad. 'All of this ... since the prom ... it's hard for me too. Not as hard as it is for you. I know that. I don't mean to …' His dad's voice falters. 'I'm just trying that's all.'

'I know,' Ram says, and carries on up the stairs.

Trying. Yeah. They were all trying.

Life had been good. Life had been right. Everything had fit properly, he'd known who he was and what he wanted to be. Now? Now none of it fit. He was broken, everything *around* him was broken, and he was supposed to just keep trying. Trying to make it all alright again. They thought he was sad, heartbroken, filled with pain and loss and all that stuff that talking was supposed to fix. He wasn't, there was sadness there, of course there was, but the main thing was anger. Rage in fact. Rage that his life, the whole perfect order of things, had been torn down. How was that right? How was that fair? None of this had been anything to do with him. Charlie? Who cared about Charlie? Just some posh kid. Some weird kid. Someone who shouldn't even have been in Ram's orbit. His problems? The stuff he was running from? None of Ram's business.

But it had been made his business. He'd been dragged into it and it had cost him Rachel, his leg and, perhaps most of all, his sense of order. Nothing fit. How that made him burn.

Now this. Some other bit of weirdness, something else that didn't fit in The World According to Ram. Something else he was being dragged into. Something they were trying to make his problem.

Trying.

Ram just wanted his life back, and all the trying in the world wasn't going to make that happen.

10

THE WALLFLOWER OF SHOREDITCH
IS COMPLETELY OFF HER HEAD

Morning, and Coal Hill School lurches into life. Kids hoist backpacks over shoulders, car doors slam and the flood towards the building begins. Give it twenty minutes, enough time for the drudgery of first period to really bed in, and the atmosphere will drop to one of mild sufferance. Now, it's all about the noise, all about the enthusiasm, in fact if you see anyone looking vaguely wary they're probably a teacher.

This is just how education works.

Obviously, the main subject of conversation is the blackened-out shell of the Collins' house, the news about which has spread virally from Wi-Fi network to Wi-Fi network. By now everyone knows, and by now everyone is thrilled.

This is just how people's minds work.

It's not evil, it's just the only way a mind can face something that awful. It is Big News. It is a ripple in the potential tedium of existence, a spike of drama that has everyone talking, fast, breathless, full of opinion, eager for grisly details.

'All of them?'

'All of them. I heard when they carried his dad out one of his arms was so burned it snapped off on the door of the ambulance.'

'No!'

'It's what I heard.'

Facts don't mean a thing the morning after, facts are speed bumps on a roller coaster of thrilling, shocking, sensational detail. Who wants to kill an amazing story with facts?

Of course, later, once the truth of it all has sunk in, once it has stopped being something so outrageous and unexpected, it will become real. Then the enthusiasm, for most, will plummet. For some it already has of course, because for some this kind of thing is already nowhere near as outrageous or unexpected as it should be.

'Do you know what happened to Max?' Tanya asks, walking along next to Charlie and Matteusz.

Charlie shakes his head. 'He's saying he didn't do it.'

'But we know he did?'

Charlie shrugs. 'They found him sat watching the house burn. Apparently his face was all singed, like sunburn, because he sat too close.'

'That is probably not true,' suggest Matteusz. 'You know what stories are like.'

'Yeah,' Tanya agrees, just about managing to control her disappointment at not being able to keep this terrifying extra detail. 'I guess.'

They head inside, the bell for registration ringing. None of them notice the dishevelled figure veering towards the front gate.

'Good morning class,' sighs Miss Quill, 'let's all pretend we can bear the thought of ploughing through this one more time shall we?' She leans on her desk and stares out of the window. All she can see is the distant playing field but, to cheer herself up, she imagines it erupting in plumes of smoke and earth, a bomb run strafing its way towards the school.

'Perhaps,' she suggests, 'we can even turn it into a little game. A game called "I Might Actually Learn Some Physics From Clever Miss Quill Today."'

'Psycho Miss Quill you mean,' someone mumbles from the back.

Quill pops the cap off a biro and onto her desk, she then flicks the cap and hits the boy who spoke bang in the centre of his forehead. This is made all the more impressive by the fact that she carries on looking out of the window while doing it.

'Oi!' he shouts. 'You can't do that! That's abuse.'

'Something you no doubt prefer doing to yourself, Mr Lowe,' she replies.

She is actually slightly angry that the round of laughter the comment generates pleases her. 'Dear God Quill,' she thinks, 'you're playing to the crowd.'

'You could have blinded me! I can report you for that!'

'And I can report you for the fact that I clearly saw you smoking a joint on the corner of the playing field half an hour ago, Mr Lowe. Shall we both report each other and see what happens?'

Mr Lowe declines to answer. Mr Lowe may be stupid but he's not blind to the notion of self-preservation.

Quill tears her eyes away from the playing field and looks at her class. 'I have empty seats,' she says, only now noticing. 'Why do I have empty seats?'

Which is when the classroom door crashes open and April stumbles in.

'Well, that's one seat accounted for,' says Quill. 'The wallflower of Shoreditch slept in. No doubt she stayed up late deciding what to name her first eight cats.'

'Ah, shut up,' April mumbles, before swinging her bag off her shoulder, tripping over it and performing an impromptu slam-down on the waste bin. 'Ow,' she moans quietly. She rolls over the now somewhat flattened bin and ends up on her back, staring up in confused pain at the strip lighting.

In any other class, this manoeuvre would have created laughter or even a round of sarcastic applause, of the sort heard in a pub when someone breaks a glass. In Quill's class, the students are genuinely unsure how badly this might play out. Considering that speaking out of turn might earn you a pen cap to the head, it seems entirely possible April MacClean may be hanging from one of the goalposts within the next five minutes. Even Quill isn't quite sure how she's going to respond as she stares at the now writhing girl. April is trying to put her bag back over her shoulder and get back on her feet. Either move seems difficult, performed together they're impossible.

Charlie's the first to respond, running over to April. She is now on her hands and knees with her bag slung over her neck.

'April, are you alright?' he asks, taking her arm.

'Absoloobly fie,' she replies, her speech so slurred it sounds like she's trying to spit out a fly that's strayed into her mouth.

'Is she … ?' Quill can barely say the words it seems so absurd. 'Is she *drunk*?'

'Of course not,' says Charlie, getting April to her feet. She turns to him, grins and kisses him. He is so startled by the sudden, violent, vodka-soaked tongue suddenly in his mouth that he just stands there, his shoulders slumped. She then vacates his face and laughs so hard that she falls over again, taking Charlie with her.

This time there is an audible inhalation of breath from the entire class. They are witnessing the best thing to happen in a classroom *ever* and none of them can quite believe it.

'She is,' says Quill. 'I don't believe it but she is. She's …'

'Completely off her head,' agrees Tanya who is now also moving to help.

'Ms Adeola,' says Quill. 'Do sit down, I can't imagine this situation is going to be improved by having three of my students flailing all over the place.'

Tanya hovers, torn between helping her friend and doing as she's told. Quill walks over to April and Charlie, tapping the latter on the shoulder as he struggles to get up, April holding onto him.

'Charles, do go away, you're not helping,' Quill says, grabbing him by the scruff of the neck and lifting him clear.

She looks down at April.

'Bit early isn't it?' she says, still not quite able to believe her own eyes. April MacClean. Miss Goody Two-Shoes. Hammered and giggling on her classroom floor.

'You're so MEAN!' April screams and then, promptly and with considerable force, throws up all over Quill's shoes.

All things considered, nobody can quite believe that April is still alive. Not only did Quill not simply snap her neck or hurl her out of the window, she actually seemed to care.

'Get on with physics,' she said. 'Read a book or something.'

Then she picked April up and half-carried her out of the room.

Now, with April sat on the closed lid of one of the student toilets, Quill is cleaning off her shoes and actually talking.

'What's this about?' she asks, but April isn't really able to answer because, in truth, she doesn't know.

Quill sighs and leans on one of the sinks. 'Seriously, Miss MacClean,' then, with a slight sigh of effort, '*April*... this isn't you, so I'm asking. Turning up to school drunk, what's that about?'

'I'm not drunk,' April says. Quill sighs again, gets up, drags April to one of the sinks and begins dowsing her with cold water, dunking her head over and over while April tries to fight back. At one point, another student walks in, a young girl from Year Eight.

'Get out,' Quill tells her. 'Use the boys' toilets if you have to, but we're busy.' The girl slowly inches out of the room and Quill goes back to dunking April.

Eventually, when both of them are soaking wet and at least one of them has had the fight knocked out of them, Quill sits April back down in one of the cubicles and resumes her position against the sink.

'So,' she says, 'where were we? That's right… I was asking why you were drunk.'

'I meant it though,' April replies. 'Of course I wouldn't drink before school. Why would I?'

'That's precisely the point of this entire conversation,' Quill replies with an irritated sigh.

'Maybe I'm coming down with something,' April says.

'Cirrhosis of the liver perhaps?' Quill suggests, wondering whether she should just start dunking April again. She knows that, generally speaking, the education system frowns on what could be perceived as physical abuse of a student, but she hasn't got it in her to care.

'I don't drink much anyway,' April says, 'I...' Truth be told she doesn't really have the opportunity, but she's not going to admit that to Quill. To develop an enthusiasm for alcohol she would need precisely the sort of social life she's never really had. 'I just don't understand it,' she replies in the end, having no other words to fall back on.

'Was it on the way to school?' Quill asks. 'I'm assuming it must be. Please tell me your mother didn't just pour it on your breakfast cereal.'

'I...' April thinks hard. 'I actually don't remember walking to school. I remember leaving the house. Said goodbye to Mum, went up the path... I saw Mr Veltham, across the road, he's weird, don't like him much...'

'This is all *so* fascinating,' Quill sighs.

'But that's it. That's all I remember, the next thing I know I'm just up the road from the school, I realise I might be late so I start running but... but it's really hard, I'm all over the place, it feels like...'

'You're drunk.'

Reluctantly, finally, April admits it. 'Yes.'

Quill stares at the ceiling and wonders if she isn't wasting her time with this after all.

'You knew the dead girl, yes?' she asks.

'Poppy? Sort of, yes. We weren't... it's not like we were close friends or anything.'

'Because it would be perfectly understandable if her death had upset you. There's been a lot of it about lately.'

'You're telling me,' April nods, sinking slightly, resting her head against the side of the cubicle.

'And I understand how that can feel.' Just saying the words makes Quill want to throw up, but it's true and, as much as she hates to admit it, there were times, on another world, in another time, when she could have really done with someone to talk to about it.

'Because of the war thing... with Charlie?'

'*Against* the little prince, not *with*, but yes, because of that.'

April nods. 'OK, yes, sorry... but honestly, this isn't that. I'm not saying I haven't been... Well, things are hard at the moment. I'm supposed to be doing exams, playing the violin, looking after Mum, not... not whatever this life we now all have is. But that doesn't mean that one morning I decide enough's enough and pour a bottle of whisky down my throat. That's just not how I deal with something like this.' She sighs. 'It's not me. For some people, when life gets too much, they become self-destructive.' She looks up and Quill is genuinely startled by the coldness she sees in April's eyes. It's a coldness she would never have imagined the girl could possess. 'I know that. I have known people like that. And it's not me. It's the very last thing I would be.'

Quill believes her. Which is awkward because, frankly, this morning would have been easier if it had been about April having a breakdown.

'So, somewhere between leaving the house and getting here, you blacked out and somehow got drunk,' she says. 'Which means we need to have you looked at by a doctor.'

'If I'd just had a blackout I'd have woken up in a hedge or something. This isn't that either.'

Quill thinks about this. 'No,' she says in the end, 'maybe it isn't.'

'In the last couple of days, two people have suddenly done things completely out of character,' April continues. 'In both cases, things that are a lot worse than getting drunk.'

'*Two* people?'

April realises that nobody has told Quill about Max. Everybody else knows, *everybody*, but nobody talks to Quill. Quill has no friends. Just for a moment, April feels a profound sadness for her.

'Last night,' she says, 'a boy set fire to his house. His family were trapped inside. He sat on the front lawn and watched it burn. By the time the firemen arrived it was too late. His mum and dad and his younger brother were all dead. It was obvious to everyone that he had done it, he had empty cans of petrol next to him, his clothes stank of

65

it. When the police arrived he told them he had no idea what had happened and that the last thing he remembered was playing on his games console.'

'Which makes me wonder if the kid that stole the car…'

'Poppy, her name was Poppy.'

'Whatever. It makes me wonder whether she would have said something similar if she had lived to walk away from it all.'

April shakes her head. 'It just doesn't stop. The weird stuff. It never, ever stops.'

'There's something else this makes me wonder,' says Quill.

'What?'

'You weren't the only one absent from the start of class. Where's Ram Singh?'

11

WHAT'S WRONG WITH EVERYTHING?

Ram wakes up and wonders what's gone wrong with the ceiling. It's dark, but not so dark he doesn't stare at the network of exposed pipes and wonder what they're doing in his bedroom. The pipes are really blurred, little more than shapes. He can't focus properly. His head is splitting, brain refusing to have a sensible thought. This is why it takes him around twenty seconds to come to the first simple truth of his situation: the pipes aren't in his bedroom, because neither is he.

He closes his eyes again and tries to make the white noise of jumbled thoughts quieten down. What's wrong with him? It's like everything's an earworm, chaotic, uncontrolled voices tripping over each other in his head.

It's like they're nothing to do with him. They are, because he recognises them: playing football with his dad, sitting on his bed watching a TV show on his laptop, running through the corridors at school trying not to die.

(And of course, Rachel's there, the look of shock on her face, the sword bursting from her chest, the wetness on Ram's face that he only later realises is her blood.)

But he's not aware of thinking these thoughts. They're just happening. Loud and clear, all at the same time, without being asked. He just needs them to shut up for a minute. To give him some peace. To give him some space. Why is he always surrounded by this mental white noise?

He opens his eyes and stares at those pipes again. They're still blurred but he fills his head with them, turning down the volume on everything else. It takes him a few moments but eventually he's clear.

'Where the hell am I?' he asks the room and that's weird because his voice sounds off, like there's something wrong with his throat.

He sits up, head quiet now but still splitting. Something's attached to it. Like a pair of headphones but with too many wires. He takes it off, throwing it onto the floor.

He's lying on some sort of couch. The sort of thing you see in movies, the sort of thing broken people lie on while they're talking to their therapist. 'No thank you,' he thinks, 'No more talking, especially not to strangers with university degrees.'

He swings his legs around so his feet touch the floor and he slowly sits up, slightly terrified at how much this will hurt his head.

He's right to worry. It's bad, a pulse of pain that nearly has him falling backwards again. It's like his head is too small to contain the pain, swelling as it builds, stopping just short of cracking open. The thing that takes his attention off it is his leg. He suddenly realises, putting pressure on his foot, that it's working properly. There's none of that slight 'offness' that he gets with the prosthetic. That niggling sensation that this is not your leg and that if you want it to do as it's told you're going to have to really concentrate.

He looks down and wonders why he's wearing a suit. Then he looks at his hands, resting on his thighs and wonders why they're white. Then he lies back down again because the world is just far too stupid today and none of this makes sense.

This is not helping.

And why can't he see properly? Why is everything so fuzzy?

Slowly he stands up and, once again, takes a second to remember what it feels like to have a leg that is entirely your own. He bounces on it slightly. Putting his weight on it. There's more weight than there should be and slowly, his pained, lagging brain starts to really catch on to all the conflicting data it's receiving. He touches his wrong, white hands to his wrong big belly and fights off a dizziness that threatens to send him right back onto his wrong fat arse.

What's going on?

He squints, rubs his face, trying to clear his vision but failing. There's a circle of ten couches like his. Only one other is occupied. A woman dressed in a bright purple dress. Ridiculously pointed high heels aim upwards like overpriced leather arrows.

He moves over to her. She looks to be asleep, her face twitching every now and then. She's wearing a headset, the same as the one he took off when he first woke up. The wires from it stretch into the pipes and he follows them using his fingers, moving to the middle of the room where they're connected to a pyramid of flashing lights and metal.

He moves over to take a look at it, stumbling slightly from the sensation of this wrong body, the way it swings, the way it hangs, the way it feels.

Seriously now. What's going on?

The pyramid is some kind of machine. He looms over it, trying to get close enough to see it properly. No visible switches, just pulsing lights dancing over a dull-chrome surface.

'I was plugged into that,' he thinks. 'And somehow it's changed me. It's turned me into…

Moving round the pyramid, he's now facing a panel that's reflective and the face looking back at him is that of a man in his fifties. Hair greying, skin pale and unhealthy, jowls hanging. He even has a moustache. A *moustache* for God's sake.

'Shut up,' he says and again, the voice is off but he can see why now, it's not his voice.

He stares at the face for quite a long time. Pulling different expressions, widening those bloodshot eyes, thinning those puffy lips. He pokes it with an index finger that shouldn't be attached to him. 'Those nails are bitten,' he thinks, 'bitten sore.' Every poke of the finger registers, he feels it. He feels the finger that isn't his touch the face that isn't his. As the concept of that really sinks in, he watches the face that isn't his pull a sneer and, finally, he recognises something of his own.

What's the last thing he can remember? And why is it *so hard* to think?

Walking. Yes. High street. Staring at the sheet of plastic plastered over the betting shop window. Police signs and bouquets of flowers. Like the dead will rest easier thanks to cheap garage-forecourt blooms. Heading to school. Yes. But not getting there. Why didn't he get there? And where's here?

He looks around again. The benches, the machine, the wires, the woman in the purple dress. Should he wake her up? Ask her what the hell is going on? Did she used to be someone else? Will she stare at her face and not know it?

Outside. He needs to find someone else. Whoever it is that's behind all this. Machines like this don't just work themselves. Someone is doing this. Someone's in charge.

He looks around for a door, but his blurred vision makes it hard. It would help if there were more lights. It would help if his head would just stop hurting.

He bumps into one of the benches, not used to moving in this body, and falls to the ground, slamming his palms on the stone floor. It hurts. These palms, hot and sore from the impact, these shoulders, jolted by the impact. Not *his* palms, not *his* shoulders and yet he gets to own the pain, how twisted is that?

Something has fallen out of his pocket ('No! Not my pocket, none of this is mine!') He picks it up and gets to his feet. It's a glasses case. He opens it, expensive designer glasses, thin metal frames. He thinks for a minute then decides, to hell with it, why not? He puts the glasses on.

Now he can see clearly. Of course he can, because this body – this old, fat, stupid body – is also short-sighted.

It makes all the difference, the door is right in front of him, a few feet away in the shadows. He walks over to it, turns the handle and is relieved to find it's not locked.

Outside he's in a narrow corridor and there's the sound of music playing to his left. Where is he? Everywhere's tatty, a brown explosion of damp on peeling, painted breeze block walls. The floor is swept clean but ancient scrape marks and the stained lines of dirty trolley wheels cut across it. Some sort of storage place? A warehouse? It looks like it hasn't seen any proper business for years but he knows that's not true because he's in it and he's not alone.

He moves towards the sound of music.

The corridor opens out into a reception area. The glass frontage has been whitewashed over so he can't see outside, can't get an idea of where this place is. In the reception area there's a single desk, a computer (that's where the music's coming from, old man's guitar rock, all power chords and Eighties synths) and a man leaning back in an office chair, his feet resting on the desk.

He has a choice.

He could ask this man what's going on. That's the obvious thing to do. Thing is, he's just woken up inside a body that's not his in a knackered old building, and what part of any of that is right? What part of it strikes you as something that should be happening? This is probably a weird experiment or something. He's not supposed to be here. He hasn't asked to be here, overweight, old and half-blind. So is talking to this bloke, this relaxing man listening to his bad music, going to make the situation worse? 'Hello mate, I wonder if you can help? I've woken up in the middle of your illegal science experiment and I was wondering if you could sort my body out and point me towards the closest bus stop?'

No. That's just not going to play, is it? That's not getting him anywhere useful.

So what does he do? Does he grab the bloke and force him to tell him? Can he even do that? He doesn't look particularly threatening. Shirt and trousers, tie slung loose. Forty? Maybe a little bit younger. He looks like a salesman for a particularly dull company. On any other day Ram would give it a go. Today, however… Today he is stuck in the body of a man that he doesn't know. He just lost a short fight with a bench. He's big but is that enough?

Ram decides it'll have to be, which is when the man sees a reflection in his computer monitor and turns around. His response is not at all what Ram expects.

'Sir!' The man jumps to his feet, knocking an empty mug off the desk causing himself a dilemma. He doesn't know what to do next, smarten himself up or pick up the mug. He tries both, the sum result of which is a man with a twisted tie holding a mug the wrong way up. 'I was told you wouldn't be up and about for at least another couple of hours, I'm so sorry.'

He suddenly remembers the music, spins round and tries to turn it off, stabbing at the keyboard short cuts, briefly making it play louder then silencing it. He turns back to face Ram who, with all of this confusion, still hasn't quite decided what to say next.

'Right,' he says and then a huge, horrible chunk of silence swells between them. Luckily for Ram, the other man comes to the rescue.

'Bit disorientated, yes?' he asks. 'It can take a good ten minutes to find your feet. That's what Mr Fletcher tells me anyway, I haven't been able to try it out myself. Not on what he pays me!' The man laughs then, but only briefly as he suddenly realises what he's said might be taken as rude. 'Which is only right, of course,' he continues, 'because Joyriders is an extremely exclusive enterprise. Obviously.' He draws to a halt and Ram finally realises that this man is just as uncomfortable in his own way as he is. Sure, he hasn't just woken up in a strange body but he's clearly terrified and if Ram can just keep it together there's a chance he can get the upper hand.

'Disorientated,' he says, just managing not to wince again and the strange sound of his new voice. 'Yeah. Very. Head's splitting actually. Can't really think straight.'

'What am I thinking?' The man grabs his desk chair and wheels it over. 'Sit down, please. Can I get you some water, maybe? I can't give you any pills or anything, for the headache, I mean, we're not allowed.' He stares down at the chair, hating how absurd it now looks stranded in the middle of the room but not knowing what else to do. 'Health and safety I suppose!' He laughs again. 'Some people are allergic, aren't they?'

Ram just nods and sits down. 'Some water would be great, thanks.'

As the man dashes over to a water cooler, faffing in panic as he realises he needs to find a fresh pack of plastic cups, Ram sits and realises he doesn't want to be there. He wants to be out of the front door and legging it up the road. Or does he? This body probably isn't going to just fall off if he runs fast enough. He needs to figure out what's happened.

The man comes back with a cup of water. 'Here you go. It's cold.' He says this as if it's the most important thing in the world, as if the temperature of the water is the glue that will bind all of his professionalism back together.

'Thanks,' Ram drinks, mainly to buy him a bit more time to think. 'Mr Fletcher…' he says in as noncommittal a way as possible, hoping it just might lead to something. It does, but it's not good.

'Yeah, he just had to pop out for a bit,' the man checks his watch. 'In fact he should be back any minute.'

Ram doesn't like the sound of that, because Mr Fletcher is obviously the boss, and there's no way he's going to be on the back foot as much as this guy.

'Right,' he says. 'Good.'

Think, Ram! Think!

Joyriders. That's what the man called this (and, of course, he can't stop the sudden image of Poppy flashing into his head, imagining her as she speeds towards that brick wall and death). That name, and the things that have happened bring an awful thought to mind. He hasn't been changed. This man doesn't think he's Ram Singh. He thinks he's someone else, he thinks he's the man who looks like this. The man who owns this body. So what does that mean? The obvious answer – and the fact that Ram even *considers* this obvious is a sign of how screwed-up his life has become of late – is that they've somehow swapped places. Like that truly horrible Ryan Reynolds movie, where he swaps with Jason Bateman. Except in the movie Bateman gets to be Ryan Reynolds and somehow decides not to have sex with Olivia Wilde. By comparison, he's stuck here drinking water with Eighties Rock wearing the body of an old guy. Life really sucks.

Is that what this is? Really? And if it is, then what the hell is old fat guy doing while he's in his body? Is he going to have anything to swap back into? Hopefully he's sleeping with Olivia Wilde.

'So,' he says, 'something obviously went wrong.'

Eighties Rock stares at him but for once says nothing.

Ram continues digging. 'You said I should have stayed asleep for another couple of hours?'

'Well, not asleep exactly, obviously, but, yeah, you paid for a full session so…' He checks his watch again. 'You should have transferred back at two o'clock.' He suddenly realises he might be fielding a customer service complaint. 'I'm sure Mr Fletcher will sort it though. You've paid for the full session and you'll get it. Definitely.'

'Great,' says Ram, trying to sound angry, which he is, just not for the reasons Eighties Rock would guess. 'Definitely. Full session. I paid, yeah?'

'Erm…' The man is looking at him. Ram wonders if he's sounding strange. This is the man's voice he's using but for all he knows the guy could have been American or something. Would he lose his accent with a different brain in place?

'Well, as long as it's sorted out,' he says, figuring he may as well keep digging as stop, 'that's fine.'

So much is going through his head, he just doesn't know what to do.

If somebody else is running around in his body he could be doing anything to it. Should he get out of here now, while he can? Or should he wait for the boss to get back so that he stands a chance of being swapped back? *Can* he be swapped back?

What should he do?

'I think I'll get a bit of fresh air,' he says. 'Maybe clear my head a bit.'

Because even if he doesn't decide to run, at least he'll then have some idea of where this is. Maybe, if they *are* swapped back, he can come back later, with a few friends in tow and see about sorting this lot out. (A few friends, yeah, like I have any of those, posh boy and the freak kids, what a great army they make.)

'Oh…' Eighties Rock clearly isn't sure about this, but he hasn't quite got the balls to flat out deny him.

'For goodness sake, man,' Ram says, trying his best to sound old and fat, 'I'm hardly going to run off am I? *You* still owe *me*, remember?'

Eighties Rock nods. 'Of course, sorry, it's just… well, you know the rules.'

'No,' thinks Ram, 'that's the problem, I don't.'

'Given what's happened,' he says, 'I think we can bend the rules a bit, don't you? I just want to clear my head a bit, is that too much to ask?'

'No, of course not, it's just… Well, Mr Fletcher is very strict about this, you know that, and if he were to know that I'd just let you go outside…'

'Well, he doesn't have to know does he?' Ram tries to offer what he hopes looks like a friendly smile. 'I won't tell him if you don't.'

But Ram has clearly found the thing that *truly* terrifies Eighties Rock: his boss. 'Sorry, but no, I really couldn't.'

Ram makes a decision. 'Fine,' he makes a run for the door, 'then you can tell him you tried to stop me.'

Eighties Rock panics but, despite Ram's awkwardness with this borrowed body, he gets to the door before he can stop him. It's just a shame that that's when Garry Fletcher steps through it.

'Oh,' Fletcher is clearly surprised to see him, 'is there a problem?'

'I told him he wasn't allowed outside, Mr Fletcher,' says Eighties Rock, desperate to cover his arse before they get down to details.

'Yeah,' says Ram, 'but I want some fresh air and I'm the paying customer here so if you don't mind getting out of my way.'

'But now that Mr Fletcher is here we can see what went wrong,' says Eighties Rock.

'In a minute!' shouts Ram, losing his cool, the half-open doorway within reach. 'First I want to get some fresh air!'

'If fresh air is what you want, Mr Spencer,' says Fletcher, 'then fresh air is what you shall have.' He stands out of the way.

Ram can't quite believe it. 'I should think so too!' he says and reaches for the door.

'Oh,' says Fletcher, 'one more thing, Mr Spencer...'

'Yes?' Ram asks, turning just in time to see Fletcher's fist raising.

'Your name,' Fletcher says. 'It's not Mr Spencer.'

12

GARRY, OLD SON, YOU JUST BECAME A MILLIONAIRE

Six months earlier.

'Yeah,' says Garry Fletcher, 'but your girlfriend's still a bit of a dog isn't she?'

Fans of intellectual debate and reasoned discourse don't often frequent the front bar of the Pig & Lettuce. There, where the carpets are bald and the bar sticky, a simpler form of interaction is favoured. Say what you like about the conversation though, a student of physics, even one of Quill's more reluctant pupils, would learn something over the course of an evening. Fletcher's comment, for example, and the punch that comes by swift reply, offer a masterclass of force in motion. Cause and effect, momentum and finally gravity are all illustrated as Fletcher sails through a

Guy Adams

small collection of bar stools and comes to rest beneath the table of an old couple.

The couple don't bat an eye when Fletcher is dragged out from between their feet and thrown through the main double doors onto the wet street outside. If pressed they would simply mutter 'No business of ours,' and look to Stan, the manager for another pint of stout and a rum and coke.

Fletcher is flat on his stomach, balancing on the lip of the kerb like a man riding the roof of a moving train. He spits blood into a puddle and decides that maybe it's time to head home.

He gets up, does his best to straighten his tie and begins limping off in search of bus stops. From experience, this is likely to be a heroic journey. He's convinced the council move the things at night. Or maybe it's Ranesh at the local kebab shop, knowing that he's bound to get hungry as he wanders lost, trying to get home.

'Ranesh,' Fletcher mutters, 'if he thinks he's getting my money tonight for doner and chips, he's out of luck.'

Of course, just the act of imagining the food, sweating together in the sauna of its polystyrene box, is enough to make him change his mind and he hovers at the corner of the street weighing up his choices.

'Excuse me?'

Fletcher looks around for the voice, not entirely convinced it's not in his head.

'Can you help me?' the voice asks and Fletcher finally pins it down. There's a kid on the other side of the street. He's ten or eleven, barefoot and dressed in a mismatched tracksuit. 'Aye, aye,' Fletcher thinks, 'this is probably trouble.' He's right, though it won't be trouble for Fletcher, not in the short term.

'You've got no shoes,' he says, shuffling across the road. 'Why've you got no shoes?' This seems the biggest problem to Fletcher and he's hoping the kid isn't going to ask to borrow his. They're cheap and the sole of the left one is now so thin the shoe could function as a lampshade, but they're his and he wants to keep them.

'That doesn't matter,' says the kid, 'I just need your help.'

'What with?' Fletcher asks, walking past the boy slightly so he can sit on the low wall that skirts the pavement. 'I haven't got any money.'

This isn't true, he's got well over a hundred quid in his pocket. It's a little private bonus that he's skimmed off the top after his usual day of flogging meat to restaurants and pubs. He sees nothing wrong in this. In fact, he's decided it's the simplest way of pleasing everybody. His boss is happy because he thinks he gets Fletcher's services for twenty grand a year, Fletcher is happy because, actually, his boss doesn't. This is simple morality in the world of Garry Fletcher.

'If you could just follow me?' The kid starts walking off down the street and Fletcher sighs. This is a pain in the arse, that's what this is. But then he wonders if the kid's lost or something. Maybe he can get a reward out of it. He gets up off the wall and shuffles along behind him.

'Where do you live?' Fletcher asks him. The kid just points, which Fletcher doesn't think is particularly helpful, especially as the kid seems to be pointing straight up into the night sky.

'Christ's sake,' he mutters, still following the kid.

After a few minutes, Fletcher's drunk enough that it all just starts to feel normal. Him and the strange barefoot kid out for a stroll. All good. One foot and then the other. No problem. He stares at the buildings around him and wonders where they're heading. They're cutting towards the little industrial estate off Swallow Avenue. He looked at a place there once during one of his frequent bouts of entrepreneurialism. What was it that time? The T-shirt printing company or the stain-proof carpet thing? Damned if he can remember, all he knows is that he didn't get the money together and that was that. That is *always* that as far as Fletcher's business empires go. You can't fault him for enthusiasm, can't even fault him for ideas, but when it comes to holding on to the cash... Well, nobody's perfect. Last he heard the industrial estate was nigh on empty, the landlord had got done for building regulations or something. Now there was just a little courtyard of abandoned buildings with peeling 'To Let' signs on them.

The kid crosses Swallow Avenue and, sure enough, aims for the narrow passageway that leads through to the industrial estate.

'I nearly rented a place here,' Fletcher says, though why he thinks the kid would be interested is anyone's guess.

'Sensors showed it was free of intelligent life,' the kid says.

'You can say that about most of Shoreditch,' Fletcher replies, before the words even really sink in. 'Wait... what?'

'It is this way.' The kid vanishes into the shadows along the estate entrance and Fletcher jogs after him. For a moment he loses the kid. He's spinning around, robbed of the streetlights, adrift in the darkness of the courtyard.

'Where did you go?' he shouts.

'Please,' says the child from right next to him, 'it would be better if you were quieter. Our records show that this planet may not welcome us, I wouldn't be talking to you if it wasn't an emergency.'

And with that, the kid walks over to one of the buildings, opens the door and steps inside.

'Off his head,' Fletcher thinks, 'completely and utterly off his head.'

But he follows anyway.

He steps inside the building just in time to see the kid heading through a dilapidated reception area and along a corridor beyond. It suddenly occurs to him that this might be a set-up, some kind of mugger's trap. 'Hang on,' he shouts, 'how about you explain what's going on here first?'

The kid stops and turns to face him. Fletcher can't see his face and right now that feels like a step too far, as if by seeing his face he could trust the kid more. 'There isn't time. Please, come.'

'No,' says Fletcher, leaning against the door. 'You explain to me what's going on or I'm leaving. Simple as. You could have load of mates in there waiting to kick my head in for all I know.'

The kid just stands there for a moment, weighing it up. 'But I need your help, you can't leave,' he says.

'So tell me what's going on. Then I'll help you. Promise.'

'We are explorers to your world.'

Fletcher laughs, but doesn't walk out, this is almost fun. 'Explorers? In what, your spaceship? Parked out back is it?'

'Our ships don't work that way. *We* don't work that way. We are . . .' the kid pauses, trying to think of the words. 'We blend.'

'Blend? What, like blend in? That's why you look like that is it? So this ship of yours is hidden or something?'

'No.' Then a pause. 'Yes, in a way. You are standing inside it.'

'This place? It's just an empty old business unit, mate, you couldn't fly this to the moon.'

'We appropriate matter. We transfer. Our sensors showed that this space was empty of intelligent life.'

'Oh yeah, you mentioned that bit.'

'So we appropriated this location,' the kid continues. 'We do not use travel structures as you would think of them. We appropriate new space, moving through space/time locations. It is still your… empty business unit but we now occupy it, along with our equipment.'

'Yeah, well…' Fletcher is heading back towards the doorway, 'this has been fun but I'm bursting for a slash and I need to get home so…' He stops, a thought bubbling up through his corrupt little mind. 'Wait, you said equipment?'

'Yes. While we do not use travel structures, we are an exploration party, we carry a great deal of scientific equipment. It is with that equipment that I need your help.'

'What sort of help?'

'I will show you, but please hurry.'

'Two ticks…' Fletcher dashes outside to empty his bladder and have a quick think. Obviously this is all rubbish, isn't it? I mean, you hear stuff these days, weird alien stuff. It's not just conspiracy nutjobs either, lots of people say they've seen things, alien things. Maybe this is on the level? Maybe?

His mind is turning over and over, trying to imagine how he might be able to profit from this.

He steps back inside. 'Right you are then, lead the way.'

The kid walks down the corridor and opens a room on the left. 'Our equipment has located itself in several of the rooms, but our power source is the main problem.'

Fletcher is staring at the huge sphere in the centre of the room and all doubt is gone. 'You are kidding me…' he whispers. 'Would you look at that?'

It glows with a pale, pearlescent light. Faint, pulsing and moving across the walls in a way that doesn't quite make sense to Fletcher's eyes. When the light reflects it seems almost to have substance, a glutinous thing that splashes onto, then drips off the walls with each pulse.

'It is failing,' the kid says. 'It has been unable to lock onto a local power source and can only last a short time in isolation.'

'A local power source?'

'We appropriate,' the kid says. 'We have occupied this space to use as our own, in the fullness of time we would bond fully with it, but to do that we need stable power.

Power from here. We understood your planet had plentiful power reserves, we would not have come here otherwise. There is not even enough to relocate. We are stranded unless we can appropriate more power.'

'And how are you supposed to do that?' Fletcher asks, walking around the sphere. 'Plug it into the mains?'

'The mains?'

'Yeah, you know, electricity.'

'Electricity would be perfect but there is none here.'

'Yeah well, they'll have been cut off won't they?' Fletcher replies.

'If there had been a source of electricity within these walls,' the kid continues. 'The sphere would have connected to it automatically. This space is dead. It has no power.'

For a moment the sphere pulses brighter.

'Wait!' the kid says. 'It has found a power source! You must have something with you? Some form of electricity perhaps?'

'Nah,' says Fletcher, then feels something glow warm in his jacket pocket. 'Oh, hang on, there's my phone I suppose.'

The sphere grows dim again. 'It is no use,' the kid says, 'there wasn't enough power in it, it has drained it already.'

'No kidding,' Fletcher is poking at his phone. 'It's dead, no battery life at all.'

'The sphere consumed it, but it was insufficient.'

'It consumed it?' Fletcher can't get his head around this. 'No wires, no nothing? It just sensed the phone in my pocket and sucked it dry?'

'We appropriate.'

'Yeah, yeah, so you keep saying. So, if I brought a generator or something into the room, this thing would just connect to it and power up? Like electricity over a Wi-Fi connection?'

'Yes. I think. I'm not sure what a Wi-Fi connection is.'

'That's amazing.'

'Thank you,' the kid actually smiles. 'So you will do that? Bring this generator?'

'Yeah, of course, as soon as you've told me what I get out of it.'

Fletcher then walks out of the room, crosses the corridor and walks straight into the room opposite. Inside there is a pyramid-like structure, again glowing with a pale light. There's a wire leading from it and into the shadows.

'Do not touch that!' the kid shouts, running in after him.

'Keep your hair on kid,' he says, 'I'm just looking. What is it then?'

'It is how I look like this.'

Fletcher is following the wire into the darkness. Digging his cigarette lighter out of his pocket he ignites it and can suddenly see what the wire is attached to. 'Jesus Christ, what's that?'

The wire extends to a flat bench, on which lies an amorphous, vaguely humanoid shape. If you sculpted a human being out of a boiled sweet then sucked on it for a bit, Fletcher imagines you'd end up with something like this.

'That is my flesh,' says the kid, 'we use the machine to appropriate other bodies. Bodies like this one.'

'But why?' Fletcher can't take his eyes of the thing in front of him. He's wondering if he might be about to bring up what remains of his night's drinking.

'Our form is not made for extreme physical exertion, so, when need be, we temporarily use others. We app—'

'Appropriate, yeah, got that. It's kind of sick. And you stole the body of this kid?'

'I needed to find someone who could help. I would have preferred someone older but with the power drain it favours the young, especially with the power drain, and this body was the closest.'

A small thought begins to grow in Fletcher's head. 'So, you can just leap into other people's bodies? Take them over?'

'Yes.'

'But I couldn't do it, could I? Because I'm human.'

'It is the machine that performs the appropriation, I am sure you could do it perfectly successfully. But there is no need, you are here, you have no need of another body.'

'And while you're in control, you can do whatever you want? That kid you're in, he can't fight back?'

'He is not even aware. We are not cruel.'

Fletcher stares at the form on the bench again. 'Poor sod. So what would happen to him if you got hurt?'

'Regrettably my consciousness is prime. If that body were damaged beyond repair, both he and I would perish. But that is not likely to happen, not now you are here. So please, can you bring this generator? There is only a short time left.'

'Yeah, yeah, one more thing.'

'Yes?'

'You keep saying we. I've only met you, where's the rest of your lot then?'

'They are in stasis. Only the pilot remains active during transfer, it saves power.'

'Stasis? What, they're asleep?'

'Yes. Inactive, until the sphere is fully powered and I consider it viable to activate them.'

'Brilliant.'

'So you will now bring us power?'

'Sort of,' says Fletcher. 'Yeah.'

Because Fletcher knows a golden opportunity when he sees one. Already his mind is calculating what he could achieve with equipment like this. It's staggering. To hell with selling meat and creaming a few quid off the top. To hell with T-shirt printing or stain-proof carpets. 'Garry old son,' he thinks, 'you just became a millionaire.'

The fact that two lives stand in the way of that bothers him not one jot. In fact, the only consideration he gives the whole thing, as he kicks the alien creature on the bench to death, is relief that it didn't take over the body of someone that might have been able to fight back.

Later, he realises it might have been a good idea to ask the alien if there was an instruction manual. Or maybe even forced it to give him a quick tutorial. That night though, with a head full of pound signs, he doesn't even give it a thought. That night is all about getting things done.

The first thing he does is take a stroll around the rest of the building, checking the other rooms, seeing what else there might be on offer. When it comes to profit, the answer is precious little, though he does briefly wonder how much he might get for the inactive alien forms he discovers in the final room off the corridor. There are four of them, hanging from a metal frame, a network of rubber pipes connecting them. Like the body in the transfer room, they have a smooth, unformed quality to them. Leaning in as close as he dare with his cigarette lighter, he tries to figure out how they work. There are dimples where eyes, nostrils and mouth should be, but no obvious break in the skin. How can they see, breathe, talk? Is everything they do done through borrowing a host body? 'Bunch of alien thieves,' he thinks, completely immune to irony. 'I've done the world a favour getting rid of them.'

It's fear that overpowers his greed in the end. What if one of them – or all of them – wakes up once he gets the power going? They don't look like much and everything he's seen suggests they can't act independently, that they would need to borrow another body to become a threat. But… But… But… It's a risk. He doesn't like the way they look either, or the way they smell: sweet but with a chemical undertone, like nail varnish remover. No. They can't stay, he'll have to deal with them. He drags the broken body of the alien and the empty, dead kid into the room and shuts the door on the problem. He'll figure it out later. But first, the power, he's got nothing unless he can sort out the power.

The scariest thing about leaving the building is the fear that somebody else might come along and take what's his. Who owns this place? Is it all still caught up in that legal mess with the landlord? Is he even remembering that right? He'll have to find out. But what about tonight? What if someone stumbles on this stuff now?

'Who's going to come here?' he thinks. 'It's abandoned, forgotten, hidden.'

But what if he's wrong?

There's nothing he can do about it, that's what gets him finally moving. He's got to go, his phone's dead, he doesn't have a car, standing here all night will get him nowhere. Still, as he jogs back onto Swallow Avenue he can't help but keep looking over his shoulder, half expecting someone to come walking along. By the time he's on a main road and hunting for a phone, he's almost crippled with panic. Someone could be raiding the place right now.

He spots an open takeaway with a phone and runs inside. He's already accepted that he needs help. He doesn't like the idea of cutting someone else in, hates it in fact, because there's not a living soul in this city he trusts, but he can't do everything by himself. He checks his pocket and finds he doesn't have any change.

'I need to use the phone,' he tells the bored Chinese girl behind the counter. 'Can you change a twenty?'

'Not unless you order something,' she tells him, waving a hand vaguely at the lit-up menu board above the counter. For Christ's sake, food is now the last thing on his mind. Still, he orders a chicken Chow Mein, takes his change and goes to the phone, while out the back someone starts hurling noodles around.

He dials, no answer. Hangs up, dials again. No answer. He looks at his watch, it's only just gone midnight, why won't Mike answer his damn phone? He dials again. Finally it's answered.

'Who's this?' asks Mike, angry but tired. 'Do you know what the bloody time is?'

'Shut up, Mike, it's Garry.'

'Garry? What do you want, man? It's gone midnight! Call me in the morning will you? I was on a late one yesterday and I'm knackered.'

'Just listen, Mike, this is serious. I need your help and there's money in it.'

There's a pause. 'How much money?'

'I will give you two hundred quid in cash if you do me this small favour, there'll be more down the line too if you want in.'

'Want in to what, Garry? This another one of your crappy business empires because, seriously man, I'm a bit tired of all that, you know?'

Normally, Garry would be tempted to tell Mike where to go with a comment like that. It was a fair point, but that doesn't mean he wants to hear it. Still, he needs him.

'This is the real deal, mate, seriously. But I need you to get moving now...'

He tells Mike what he wants, grabs his chicken Chow Mein and runs back to Swallow Avenue.

Heading into the courtyard, he's looking around for sign of life but the place is as dead as earlier. Inside the building, all is as he left it, so he heads back out to Swallow Avenue, sits on a wall and eats his takeaway while waiting for Mike to show up. Considering he hadn't even wanted it, it goes down at lightning speed and he feels all the better for it. By the time Mike does pull up, half an hour or so later, he's sober and got his swagger back.

He waves for Mike to turn into the courtyard, all the while wishing the man's van was a bit quieter. Hopefully everyone's in bed, the last thing he wants is twitching curtains from nosy neighbours. If anyone is looking, Mike's van is hardly subtle, 'Sparkz Mobile Disco' it announces, with Mike's phone number stencilled underneath.

Mike gets out of the van. Fletcher notices that Mike has shaved his head again. Mike thinks it makes him look cool, but he hasn't got the head shape for it, he just looks like an ugly egg.

'Turn your lights off and keep quiet,' Fletcher tells him. 'We don't want people to see us.'

'See us doing what?' Mike asks, though he reaches into the cab and flicks the lights off. 'You got my money?'

'In a minute, Mike, Jesus, just get the gear and follow me, would you?'

'Money first.'

Fletcher swears under his breath and takes out a hundred quid from his wallet. 'Hundred now, I'll draw some more out when I get to a cash machine.'

'Typical, you promised me two hundred and you haven't even got it on you.'

'Take the bloody money, I'll sort you the rest. Anyway, once you see what's going on in here you won't be fussing over a few quid, there's plenty more where that came from, I'm telling you. I wouldn't be doing all this otherwise.'

Mike takes the money and, muttering to himself, opens the back doors of the van. Fletcher winces at the sound of the heavy doors banging open but there's not much that can be done about it.

'You'll have to help me,' Mike tells him. 'It weighs a tonne and one of the front wheels sticks.'

Together they sort out a short ramp from the flatbed of the van to the ground and then Mike climbs into the van to guide the generator onto it. It's a big red and black rectangle, three feet or so wide. It has handles on the back and wheels on the front so it can be shifted like a wheelbarrow. Between the two of them, they get it onto the ground.

'There's spare petrol in the back,' says Mike. 'And you'll owe me for that as well, don't forget.'

'Yeah, yeah…' Fletcher grabs the extra cans of petrol and leads Mike inside. He's hoping this thing will do the trick, at least until he can figure out a more permanent solution. Mike uses the generator whenever he does outdoor gigs, apparently it can kick out about 230 volts going full tilt and a full tank keeps the thing going for hours.

'What is this place anyway?' Mike asks as Fletcher leads him to the room with the sphere in it.

'Nothing,' Fletcher tells him. 'It's what's inside that's interesting.'

He has a sudden thought. 'You got your phone on you?'

'Course I have, why?' Mike narrows his eyes. 'You going to start running up a bill on *that* now are you?'

'I wish you'd stop moaning, Mike, I'm doing you a major favour here, you'll see. Just leave your phone out here, it'll get drained otherwise.'

Mike starts muttering again but does as he's told. That's the best thing about Mike, Fletcher thinks, he may be a moaner but when it comes down to it, he does what you tell him.

Leaving the phone on the dusty desk in what used to be the reception area, Mike follows Fletcher. He pushes the generator down the corridor and turns it into the sphere room.

He stops on the threshold. 'What the hell is that thing, Garry?' he asks.

The sphere is barely lit now, and Fletcher knows they need to get moving. Who knows what will happen if the power runs out completely?

'Just get the generator going, quick as you can, you'll see.'

Mike doesn't argue, he just keeps staring at the sphere, can't take his eyes off it in fact, as he cranks the generator up.

'Run it at a low output for now,' says Fletcher. 'Whatever the minimum is.'

Mike nods and then stumbles back as the sphere starts pulsing brighter, feeding off the generator. 'What's it doing?' he asks. 'It's not going to blow up or something is it?'

Fletcher hasn't thought about this as a possibility but can't see why it would. When you're clever enough to build a machine like this surely you're clever enough to make sure it doesn't explode.

'It's feeding off the power from the generator,' he tells Mike.

'Can't be,' says Mike, 'I haven't plugged it in.'

'Doesn't need plugging in,' Fletcher explains, 'it just drains whatever's close by, that's why I told you to leave your phone outside.'

Mike shakes his head, not able to understand any of this. 'This some sort of prank thing, Garry? You having a laugh with me or what? Cos if you are I'll kick your head in, you know that?'

'No prank. You are looking at an alien power device.'

'Alien?' Fletcher has been prepared for the tedious explanations of this, but it turns out they're not necessary. 'That explains it I suppose,' says Mike.

'You believe in aliens?' Fletcher asks. He hears the incredulous tone in his voice and realises he's being stupid. After all, so does he now.

'Course I do. Who with an ounce of common sense doesn't?'

Fletcher laughs, the bit he thought would take major convincing is done in a heartbeat. Not that it would have been difficult. He was going to take Mike down the corridor and let him take a look at the … The other aliens! What if the power is waking them up?

'You got your tools in the van, Mike?' he asks.

'Yeah,' Mike's voice has gone dreamy, staring at the sphere as it pulses ever brighter, its liquid light splashing all over the walls. 'Alien power source, can you believe it?'

Fletcher is already running back out to the van. He pokes around in the back and finds a crowbar and long-handled lump hammer. Perfect. He runs back inside, dragging Mike out of the sphere room on the way.

'What's the problem now?' Mike asks. 'Something else need fixing?'

'You could say that,' Fletcher hands him the crowbar. 'I still haven't told you how I found this place. I was dragged here by one of these aliens wasn't I?'

'Seriously?'

'Seriously.' Fletcher's thinking on his feet but that's OK, he's good at that. 'It had changed its shape to look like a human kid.'

'Freaky.' Mike's nodding and Fletcher's loving every minute. As soon as it comes down to aliens, this div is putty in his hands.

'It tried to kill me, wanted to do experiments on me or something.'

'Experiments on *you*?' Now Mike sounds incredulous, like it's fine until Garry Fletcher is chosen as a prime example of the human race.

'Yes Mike,' Fletcher replies, grip tightening on the lump hammer. 'On *me*, got a problem with that?'

Mike shrugs. 'So what did you do?'

'Only thing I could do, I killed it.'

'You killed an alien?' Mike is floundering now and Fletcher knows he has to work to get him back onside.

'Yes I did, because it was it or me. And now we need to protect ourselves again, because there's a bunch of them on the other side of this door and if they attack we're screwed. For our sake – no, for *everyone's* sake – we need to deal with them, and quick.'

'There are aliens on the other side of this door?'

'Mike, I need you to focus for me here. You trust me, yeah?'

'Not really, mate, no. You've never given me any reason to have you?'

Fletcher supposes he's got a point. 'Doesn't matter, I mean, thanks a lot, but I need you to help me with this. These things are dangerous and right now it's down to us to deal with them.'

'Screw that, we could just call the police.'

'No! That's the last thing we do.'

'Why?'

'Because this way we get to save the world and get really, really rich. If we call the police then we walk away with nothing.'

'What do you mean really, really rich?' Mike's wavering, he's not an idiot, he can feel the lure of cash like anyone.

'I mean millionaires, Mike, seriously, there's stuff here, stuff we can just *take*, that will mean we are seriously minted for life. Why should the government get it, eh? Cos that's what will happen. The powers that be will just roll in and take everything. Why should we let them have it when we can solve the problem and keep it for ourselves?'

Fletcher thinks for a minute.

'Tell you what,' he says, 'don't worry about it. I'll just do it on my own. I'll bung you your two hundred quid, I'll even throw in another hundred for the petrol. You stay out here and I'll just make this my business, alright? I thought you'd want in but it doesn't matter, I can handle it on my own from here so you just wait outside and I'll be with you in a minute.'

'Well, hang on…'

'No mate, seriously, you're obviously not up for it. That's fine. No skin off my nose. In fact, brilliant, I don't have to share! I don't want you involved, get out.'

'That's typical of you that is,' says Mike, 'I'm alright Jack, sod everyone else. Nah, I'm not being dragged out of bed in the middle of the night then being fobbed off, shoved out of the way.'

Mike pushes Fletcher to one side and moves to open the door. Fletcher's enjoying this but he reckons one final nudge is probably best. He grabs Mike and pulls him back.

'Not a chance, I gave you the choice and you made it. This is nothing to do with you now, you can sod off out of it.'

Mike hauls him up against the wall, sneering face pushed right up into Fletcher's. 'I said no, Garry, alright? You're not cutting me out of this, you get me?'

Fletcher gives it a moment then nods with feigned reluctance. 'OK, fine, we're in this together.'

They open the door and walk inside. Fletcher has been right to worry, where before there had been darkness, now lights are flowing across the metal frame, the rubber piping flexing of its own accord. The four aliens are clearly showing signs of life, their glistening, tubular limbs slowly flexing and twisting, their ill-formed heads rolling on barely discernible necks.

'Jesus, Garry,' says Mike, 'just look at them!'

'I know,' says Fletcher, 'disgusting ain't they?'

And he starts swinging with the lump hammer, pounding into them as if they're nothing but a partition wall they need to clear. Skin bursts. Pale blue, glutinous blood sprays in great arcs across the room. That sweet smell gets stronger by the second. Fletcher stops and stares at Mike. 'Well?'

Mike pauses for a moment then joins in, swinging the crowbar. Between the two of them, the place is a charnel house in seconds.

'Job done,' says Fletcher, pulling Mike out of the room. He hasn't noticed the body of the kid because Fletcher was careful to shove it in the furthest corner, beneath the body of the alien. Fletcher thinks that, for now, it's best to leave it that way. Smashing up weird-looking aliens is easy. Dealing with the sight of a dead kid? That might give Mike cold feet again and Fletcher's too tired to be bothered with it.

They look down at the state of themselves, clothes dripping with that thick, syrupy stuff the aliens have for blood.

'Bit of a state,' Fletcher says.

Mike's face is slightly vacant, he's retreated inside himself to deal with this. After a moment it's as if he hears what Fletcher has said. 'Think I've got some wet-wipes in the van.'

There's a pause and then Fletcher starts laughing and, for a while, just can't stop.

This was the first day of the rest of his life.

13

SCHOOL, FOOTBALL, PRACTICE, HOME

Now the idea that Ram might be in trouble has taken seed, it's growing and it's impossible to concentrate on anything else. After Quill finally manages to dismiss the rest of her class, she lets April tell the others what they talked about in the toilets. It's vague, it means nothing, but fear for Ram gives it weight.

'We need to try and find him,' says Charlie.

'You can't just leave school,' says Quill, 'it's a rule.' She is immediately furious with herself for saying this. The Warrior Queen is worrying about someone getting detention slips. 'OK,' she continues, 'forget I just said that. This irritating life is obviously getting to me.'

'So what should we do?' asks Charlie. 'Where does Ram go?'

'School, football practice, home,' says Tanya. 'That's all I really know.'

'He must do more than that,' April replies.

'He probably does but you don't actually know him that well do you?' says Quill. 'If it wasn't for the fight with Corakinus you wouldn't be talking to him at all.'

There's silence at that, because, awkwardly, they know it's true. Ram wasn't friends with them before the prom, in fact nobody's really sure he's friends with them now.

'We should check the playing field,' says Tanya. 'Just in case.'

Quill is about to tell her there's no point. Why would Ram come to school and then just hang around on the playing field? Then she realises she hasn't a better suggestion of where to look, so keeps her mouth shut.

'Maybe we'll see someone there that knows him,' suggests Charlie, 'or has a better idea of where he might go when he's not—'

'Hanging around with you lot fighting monsters?' interrupts Quill. She shrugs. 'Everyone needs a hobby.'

'And what are you going to do?' Charlie asks her.

'I could say it's nothing to do with me,' says Quill, taking some small pleasure in how Charlie's face sours, 'but then I know you'll only go on. So, I'll speak to his father.'

'And say what?' asks April.

'I'm very clever, I'll think of something.'

Quill walks into the school office and straight into the path of Veronica Cutler, one of the teaching assistants. Quill does not like Veronica Cutler. Granted, Quill doesn't like anybody, but she reserves a special quantity of bile for this whining, intrusive creature. She is all about brightly coloured clothing, theatrical affectation and gossip. Being in her company is like having to share a very small cupboard with a very bright light bulb.

'Excuse *me*,' says Veronica, as if this near miss is one of the greatest affronts she has ever had to face. 'Is the school burning down?'

'Sadly not,' Quill replies, wishing that, just for a moment Veronica could see what Quill really looked like before she was buried beneath this dull, soft suit of human skin. She imagines it would make Veronica scream. She loves the idea of Veronica screaming. 'Where's the secretary?' she asks.

'Who can tell?' Veronica sighs. 'She's never around when you need her. The whole place is going to hell as far as I can see.'

'I agree,' says Quill, moving over to the secretary's desk and sitting down in front of her computer. She hates computers, especially Earth computers. Earth has really mastered the technology of making computers pretend to be efficient while actually being the exact opposite. When you shout at them they don't even answer back.

'I'm not sure you're supposed to do that,' says Veronica, watching Quill as she stabs at the computer keyboard with her finger, like someone hunting for pressure points and the pain they will cause. 'It probably breaches some rule or another.'

'Do you really care?' Quill asks, finally managing to open up the student database and scanning through it for Ram's information.

Veronica thinks for a moment. 'No,' she says eventually, with the gravity of a royal edict, 'I don't think I do. I mean, what with everything else, that fuss at the prom, the frightful business with the Sports Department.'

'Frightful.' Quill knows all she has to do is pretend to be listening.

'And Coach Dawson was so delicious to look at, I thought,' Veronica has a dreamy look on her face now. 'All those lumps and bumps. And I swear he never wore a pair of underpants in his life, shorts and tracksuit bottoms bulging and flicking in the most startling manner.'

'Really?' Quill has found Ram's information and is reaching for the phone so she can call the daytime number listed. If there's one thing she hates more than Earth computers it's Earth communications devices. After all, whenever you use one you end up talking to a human. It rings for a few seconds and is then answered by the receptionist at Ram's father's dental surgery.

'I used to be quite hypnotised at times,' continues Veronica, seemingly oblivious to the fact that Quill is trying to make a phone call. 'Watching the movement in those tracksuit bottoms. It was like the pendulum on a grandfather clock.'

'Hello,' says Quill, doing her best not to just scream down the line, 'I need to speak to Mr Singh, it's Miss Quill from Coal Hill School.'

'And as for when he went jogging…'

'I am trying to make a phone call, you chattering sack of hormones!' Quill shouts, then immediately apologises to the receptionist. 'Sorry, yes, it's about his son.'

'Well,' says Veronica, 'if you're going to be like that.' She storms out and Quill breathes a sigh of relief. Varun Singh comes on the phone.

'Hello, is there a problem?' Quill can hear the panic in his voice and tries her very best to sound warm and charming to put him at ease. This is completely outside her skillset. She excels at fighting, killing and guerrilla warfare. Warmth and charm were never things she had to learn.

'So sorry to disturb you, Mr Singh,' she says, 'please don't worry, I'm sure everything's fine, this is Ram's physics teacher, Miss Quill.'

'Oh,' he says, 'I've heard about you.'

What is that tone in his voice, Quill wonders, and what exactly has Ram been telling him about her?

'Is my son OK?' he asks again.

She decides to be honest. 'That's why I'm calling. He didn't attend my lesson today and, as I know he's been going through a difficult time...'

'That's one way of putting it,' he says.

Does he know? thinks Quill. Has Ram actually told him what's been going on?

'I just wondered if he'd stayed at home today?' she asks.

'I had to leave the house early, but I don't think so.'

That panic is still there, Quill hears it clearly, he *does* know. That's not the sound of a father that thinks his son might just be skiving off, that's the sound of a father that thinks his son might be in danger. She's not sure how she feels about that. She and Charlie are supposed to be hiding, she doesn't want the whole damn world knowing who she is. Is this man going to be a problem? A threat?

'I'm sure there's nothing to worry about,' she says, more, if she's honest, because she doesn't want him turning up at the school and kicking up a load of fuss.

'Are you now?' says Varun. 'Well, I'm not. Have you tried to call him?'

'He's not answering,' she admits. There's a pause and she hears him sigh down the phone.

'I'll cancel the rest of my appointments today and see if I can find him,' he says before hanging up.

'You do that,' Quill tells the dead line and hangs up herself.

Varun gives the busy waiting room a half-glance and then offers a guilty smile at the receptionist. 'You're not going to like this…'

Charlie, April and Tanya are walking towards the playing fields, doing their very best to make it appear as if they have every right to be doing so.

'Anything could be happening to him,' says Tanya, 'or his mum or dad!' She suddenly panics as this thought occurs to her. 'What if they make him kill his parents?'

'Why would they?' says April, then thinks of the Collins family and realises she has no useful argument to offer.

'Quill's calling them,' says Charlie. 'She'll find out if they're OK.'

'I'm going to try Ram again.' Tanya takes out her phone and dials. After a few seconds she hangs up again. 'Still no answer,' she says, to the surprise of none of them.

April sighs. 'What Quill said, about us not really being his friends, that's kind of true isn't it?'

'I've tried,' says Charlie, 'I've been nice. And he's knocked my school books out of my hand.'

'He doesn't mean it,' says April. 'Probably.'

'Of course he does,' Charlie replies. 'He doesn't like me. That's OK, I don't need him to.'

'I'm his friend,' says Tanya. 'Well, a bit, I help him with his homework occasionally.' She realises she's probably not supposed to tell them that so she tries to dismiss it. '*Very* occasionally.'

'There you go then,' says April. 'Quill was right.'

'She often is,' says Tanya.

'Which shows you don't know her like I do,' Charlie replies.

Turning to glance behind them, something catches his eye. 'Is that…' he squints, 'is someone on the roof of the school?'

April and Tanya turn and look.

'Oh God,' says April, 'what now?'

* * *

Arriving back home, Varun still hasn't decided when he's supposed to call his wife. He knows that it's not his place to tell her what's been happening to Ram, but he also knows that Ram doesn't understand quite how difficult that is. To Ram it's a shared confidence, with no question that his dad should tell anybody else, but he can only see his parents as just that: parents. Ever since Varun has known about what happened at the prom, what happened to his son's leg, he's been forced to keep that secret from his wife, the woman he loves. He knows that if – probably when – she finds out, Janeeta will find it hard to understand how he could have done that.

Ram has insisted that it's all done with, a weird, impossible moment that he's now getting over and moving on from. But if that's true then where is he now? Has something else happened? Something else that Varun cannot even begin to get his head round? And if that possible thing that might (or, please, *please* might not) have happened has harmed their son further, will Janeeta ever forgive him for keeping the truth from her?

He goes inside the house and calls for his son. Of course, there is no answer. He goes upstairs anyway, foolishly convincing himself that Ram is just wearing his headphones and hasn't heard him. When he opens the bedroom door he'll be lying there on the bed, safe and sound. He probably felt ill today, or maybe just couldn't face going to school (how that would have made Varun angry only a few hours ago, what a great relief it would be now).

He opens the bedroom door. It's empty.

So when does he call his wife?

Access to the school roof is supposed to be locked, with keys only granted to the caretaker and necessary maintenance staff. When Charlie, April and Tanya arrive at the top of the stairs they find the door has been forced and is hanging open, the slight breeze rattling it in its frame.

'Shouldn't we tell someone?' asks Tanya. 'We'll get in trouble for going out there.'

Charlie looks at her, his eyebrows raised. 'He can look so old sometimes,' she thinks.

'We should check what's happening first,' says April. 'It could just be someone messing about.'

'No,' says Charlie, 'it isn't.' And neither of them can disagree.

They step outside and the breeze that had seemed gentle on the ground is twice as forceful up here.

Moving past the access door they see a figure in school uniform over to their left. Tanya recognises him.

'That's Amar,' she says. 'I used to be in the same year as him. He's nice.'

'Great,' says April, 'then why don't you go and ask the nice boy what he's doing up here?'

'OK,' says Tanya, now entirely full of confidence as she strolls out across the roof to the boy who is staring over the low railing and looking down on the road beneath. 'Amar!' she shouts. 'What are you doing up here?'

He turns slowly and she's relieved to see he's smiling. 'If he's that happy,' she thinks, 'this can't be that serious.'

'What did you call me?' he asks.

'Amar,' she replies. 'That's your name, isn't it?' she laughs, though she'd be lying if she said the question hasn't thrown her. 'Amar Sai, I used to be in your class, remember?'

'Amar,' he says, still smiling. 'Nice name. Not mine though.'

'OK, what is your name then?' Tanya can hear Charlie and April coming up behind her and she's glad of the fact. Amar's clearly not himself and, given everything that's happened, she's suddenly not feeling as confident any more.

'Viola,' Amar says, 'Viola Cummings, what's yours?'

'Viola?' asks April. 'But that's a girl's name.'

'Yes,' says Amar, 'it is, isn't it?'

Charlie decides that maybe it's best to play along. 'So what are you doing up here, Viola?'

'I was thinking about jumping off, actually.'

'Jumping off!' Tanya is close enough to the edge to get a sense of how high up they are and the thought makes her sick. 'Why would you want to do that?'

'I thought it might be useful.'

'Nothing useful about killing yourself,' says April and there's a weight to her voice that shows this is something she knows a little about.

'Oh, but it wouldn't kill me,' says the boy who looks like Amar. 'Not this time anyway. I was looking at it as a trial run. Just to see how it felt. To see if it was something I could do.'

'If you jump off there,' says Charlie, 'you won't get a second chance to try it.'

Amar shrugs. 'Shows what you know, my dear.'

My dear? What kid speaks like that?

'Are you sure it's tall enough?' asks Tanya, and both Charlie and April can't quite believe *that's* what she's choosing to bring to the conversation.

'Of course it's tall enough,' says Amar. 'This body wouldn't survive that.'

This body?

'Probably not,' Tanya admits, 'but you'd certainly feel it and it wouldn't be nice. You speed up as you fall, faster and faster until you reach terminal velocity, which, by the way, for a human body is usually around fifty-four metres per second.'

'That's very fast,' says Amar.

'Yeah, but you wouldn't get anywhere near that at this height,' say Tanya, 'not even close, there's just not enough room to accelerate.'

'You're very strange,' says Amar, turning to look over the small railing again, which is when Charlie grabs him and tries to yank him back. It's a brave thing to do but also a bit stupid. Amar is too close to the edge and Charlie's feet slip slightly on the gravel. He just hasn't got the force to pull him back. They both end up falling towards the edge.

'Charlie!' April tries to grab hold but Charlie is moving too fast, her fingers catch at his shirt and nothing else as he falls forward.

Amar hits the rail and momentum carries him over, pulling Charlie with him. Charlie manages to wedge himself against the rail, rolling over so he's straddling it. He's still holding Amar tightly by the arm. Charlie cries out as the weight of the kid's body threatens to dislocate his shoulder.

'Oh,' says Amar, scrabbling at the corner of the roof, the rubber soles of his shoes squeaking and sliding on the glass surface of the side of the building. The boy calling himself Viola Cummings, so calm up until now, looks panicked. 'Maybe not,' he says. 'No maybe not.'

He fights to get a grip on the low railing as both April and Tanya grab hold of Charlie, trying to pull him back. 'Grab hold of him!' Charlie shouts. 'He's breaking my arm!'

April, lying flat over Charlie manages to do just that, yanking at Amar's uniform jacket and getting a grip on his arm.

'I don't like it!' Amar shouts. 'I don't like it!'

'Whose fault is that?' Tanya screams, holding on to Charlie and pressing her feet against the railing to use her legs as leverage.

Slowly, painfully, they manage to pull the boy back over the edge of the roof, all falling back onto the gravel in pained exhaustion.

'No,' says Amar, 'I don't think that's how I want it to end.'

And then he bursts into tears.

14

THE JOY OF BEING GARRY FLETCHER

There is nothing Garry Fletcher likes more in life than being Garry Fletcher. It is, by any worthwhile standard, an amazing thing to be. The fact that he's really good at it is the icing on the cake.

'Keep the change,' he tells the girl behind the cafe counter, not because he's generous but because he thinks she's hot. He turns away just in time to miss her false smile turn into a slight sneer as she eyes the seventy pence he has graced her with. It's easy to remain confident if you don't pay attention to other people.

He takes his coffee to a table in front of the window and looks out at the panoramic view of his city. That's how he thinks of it, *his* city, because his ego is even taller than the building he's drinking in. If you wanted to clock the view from the summit of Garry Fletcher's ego you would need oxygen equipment.

It had been an early start today, trying to fit in his ever-expanding client list, but he'd done the meet-and-greet and Steve could handle the rest. Steve has been an absolute godsend for business. He's solid and dependable and, best of all, seems to have zero interest in what Fletcher and Joyriders actually does. Obviously, he has a vague idea of the basics but seems to think it's just some 'VR thing' and Fletcher has been happy to leave it at that. He still doesn't like employing staff, not after that business with Mike, but he can't handle everything on his own. Besides, he has to trust his clients, so what does one more person matter? He's made Steve fully aware of the contractual elements of working for him ('Breathe a word and it'll be the last breath you take') and beyond that, he secures his loyalty with cold hard cash. The sort of money he's paying Steve is the sort of money you don't want to lose. Fear and greed, you can run a country by encouraging that attitude, so why not a business?

Fletcher takes a sip of his coffee and removes from his pocket the small black notebook he's taken to carrying. He's become far too paranoid to keep any information about the business on his computer and has decided old school pen and ink is the way to go. The fact that someone could steal the notebook has never occurred to him, Fletcher is inconsistent with his paranoia.

He scans through the list of clients booked in for the next few weeks. There's the investment banker with all the enthusiasm for kink but none of the nerve. The movie producer who just 'wants to *feel* something, you know?' The journalist who, if previous experience is anything to go by, will spend three hours with a new body, new underwear and a full length mirror. The importer who likes nothing more than taking out his week's stress on someone else's face with someone else's knuckles. The ambassador for… well, Fletcher can never quite remember… who will scoff his way through enough drugs to make a rhinoceros smile briefly, before slipping into a coma…

It's one hell of a list of clients and it goes on and on and on.

Fletcher is surprised by some of the requests. He imagined most people would just want to sleep around for a bit on someone else's conscience, but maybe that says more about him than anything else. Lots of his clients don't even do anything that illegal, they just want to feel what it's like to wear a younger body again. To be able to run as fast and as far as only eighteen-year-old lungs can. He has one client who will spend her entire allotted time just trying on clothes she can no longer fit into herself. It's kind of sad really.

But then he has the serious cases. He knows he really needs to start limiting those, not for any moral reason (Fletcher couldn't care less about some teenager he doesn't know) but because people will really start to talk. He doesn't for one minute think anyone could trace what's going on back to him. Who would believe it? But the equipment has its limitations. The further afield you search, the younger the transplants need to be and, even then, it struggles to pick anything up once you're outside a mile or two. God knows why, add it to the list of 'Things I Should Have Asked That Alien Before I Kicked It To Death.' It's a narrow playing field and if he's not careful, it'll get to the point when the area is in such panic and under such close scrutiny, nobody will want to play.

But those serious clients do know how to pay big.

To begin with he made a point of total anonymity. He didn't want to know what people got up to, it turned his stomach half the time. He also assumed clients wouldn't want to tell him. Surely the whole idea of this was to be able to get away with murder (literally if you so wished)? To do things that you'd always dreamed of doing, to act out your deepest fantasies. That was the sort of personal stuff Fletcher wouldn't dream of telling anybody. But most of his clients had surprised him, they couldn't wait to relive it all. Fletcher finally realised it was because of his own rules. He'd made it clear that clients weren't allowed to disclose anything about his business or what he got up to. Obviously. But that meant they had nobody to share it with *and people loved to share.* He'd started to factor in an extra hour after all sessions, just because he knew that most of them would want to tell him about every punch they'd thrown, every person they'd slept with (and how, and for how long), every item they'd nicked, smashed or eaten. He was their father confessor and best friend all rolled into one.

He'd hated it to start with but, after a few days, it all became the same old drone. He'd smile and make the right noises, let them think they'd shocked him (because so many wanted that, they wanted to think they'd acted completely beyond the pale). Soon he even began to find it boring.

Sometimes it had been useful, though, and given him an idea what people really wanted. He'd held one client while they'd sobbed about slashing their wrists in the bath. 'If only I had the guts to do it for real,' they'd said, dousing the shoulder of his suit jacket in tears and snot. 'Why can't I just be a real man and kill myself?' It hadn't taken Fletcher more than a few seconds to see the opportunity there. If this guy wanted someone to kill him he was sure, for a fee, he could arrange it. After all, he had another client that was clearly muscling up to kill someone, so he'd just organised accordingly. He'd been able to charge the assassin and the victim for the privilege, easy money!

One client who always kept his mouth shut was old O'Donnell, the man booked in that very morning. In fact he paid extra for the privilege, at his own insistence. He'd turn up, pay his money and then go off 'fishing' as he called it. Three hours later he'd be back in his own body and would walk out without saying a word. Fletcher assumed he must be up to something really nasty, but being a regular who paid over the odds, he wouldn't dream of pushing it. Let O'Donnell do whatever he wanted, as long as it didn't come back to bite Fletcher on the arse he couldn't care less.

Garry Fletcher finishes his coffee, puts his notebook away and heads back to the office.

He's just stepping inside the building when he comes face-to-face with O'Donnell. He shouldn't be up and about for at least a couple of hours.

'Oh,' Fletcher says, surprised, 'is there a problem?'

'I told him he wasn't allowed outside, Mr Fletcher,' says Steve. Which is true, he doesn't want people hanging around outside for one thing, for another, he doesn't want people to figure out where he is. Never trust a client, that's what he thinks, they could come back here mob-handed and try and take all this away from him. All the clients are picked up, blindfolded and driven straight to the courtyard outside. They're then led in here, where all the windows are painted-out. Then, and only then, do they have the blindfolds taken off.

'Yeah,' says O'Donnell, 'but I want some fresh air and I'm the paying customer here so if you don't mind getting out of my way?'

There's something wrong about O'Donnell, Fletcher decides. The way he's carrying himself and the way he speaks. It's O'Donnell's body and O'Donnell's voice but it doesn't seem like O'Donnell. Steve's talking but Fletcher's not listening, he's trying to decide if his gut instinct about this is right.

'In a minute!' shouts O'Donnell, and this is definitely not like him. O'Donnell is quiet. O'Donnell hasn't raised his voice once in the time Fletcher's known him. 'First I want to get some fresh air!'

'If fresh air is what you want Mr Spencer,' says Fletcher, having made a decision, 'then fresh air is what you shall have.' He stands out of the way, intrigued to see how this plays out and, right enough, 'O'Donnell' doesn't bat an eyelid at Fletcher getting his name wrong. He just nods and heads for the door. But maybe he wasn't paying full attention, Fletcher has to be completely sure, this client alone is *en route* to making him a millionaire, he doesn't want to lose him.

'I should think so too!' 'O'Donnell' says.

'Oh,' Fletcher replies, 'one more thing, Mr Spencer.' This time he's put real emphasis on the name, there's no way the man could have missed it.

'Yes?' the pretend O'Donnell says, turning to face him.

'Your name. It's not Mr Spencer.' Fletcher decks him one.

'Oh my God!' Steve is really panicking now.

'Just help me,' Fletcher says, grabbing the false O'Donnell and putting him in a neck hold. 'This isn't our client.'

'What do you mean it's not our client?' asks Steve, still panicking, hopping from one foot to the other. Then the penny seems to drop. 'Oh!'

'Help me with him!' Fletcher says and as he's squeezing the man's neck tightly, he can feel the strength slipping from him. He's got to be careful here, he doesn't want to kill O'Donnell, that wouldn't help anyone in the long run. He needs to look after this body so O'Donnell has got somewhere to return to, that way he can keep him on as a client and they still have a chance to make this mess go away.

He lets go of the man's neck. He's not a brilliant fighter but he knows a trick or two. One of his mum's first boyfriends had been a squaddie and he'd shown Fletcher stuff when the two of them were on their own. He knows you have to be careful with a chokehold, you're much more likely to kill someone than knock them out, whatever you see in the movies. Still, he thinks he's got away with it, the big man is slumping to the floor.

'Grab his legs!' he tells Steve and, between them, they drag the body back to the transfer room.

They drop him on his couch and Steve starts fiddling with the transfer headset while Fletcher moves to the pyramid at the centre.

He glances over at Mrs Cummings. 'Bless her,' he thinks, 'she does enjoy her Tuesday morning ballet class.'

'He's hooked up,' says Steve, and Fletcher starts pressing at the lit sections on the machine. It took him a few weeks to figure this out and, even now, he's never quite sure what he's doing. When you're operating it you can often feel the machine itself talking back to you in your head, like it knows what you're trying to do and is, in a limited way, guiding you. On one side of the pyramid it shows a local map so you scan for a suitable body, you select one then transfer. That body is held, a blinking light, on a different side of the pyramid. When you wanted to reverse that transfer, you hit the active light and the machine swaps them back.

The light isn't there.

'Oh, don't start...' Fletcher moves around the machine, trying to see if it's moved elsewhere. Maybe O'Donnell's body waking up has disrupted the connection somehow.

The light definitely isn't there.

'Are you doing it, Mr Fletcher?' Steve asks and Fletcher is a few deep breaths away from punching him.

'There's something wrong,' he admits and Steve looks really panicked then. Later, Fletcher will think back on that moment and realise he should have read more into that look but, for now, he's so occupied with the single problem in front of him, it passes him by.

'Think, think...' He moves around the pyramid again. Definitely no light.

There's a low groan from O'Donnell's body.

'I think he's waking up Mr Fletcher,' says Steve.

Oh, this is just getting too much. He should just kill O'Donnell now and make the whole problem go away. But Fletcher really doesn't want to lose the money. He makes a decision.

'I need to think how to sort this out. For now we lock him up.'

'Lock him up?'

'Just grab his bloody legs again, will you?'

They pick O'Donnell's body up and Fletcher guides them back out into the corridor and towards the room at the far end. The only room with a lock.

'In there?' Steve looks worried; he knows he's not allowed in this room, it's another one of the rules. Fletcher's actually slightly pleased by that. See? All you've got to do is scare your staff, then they'll always do as they're told.

'Just help me get him to the door, then you can go and check on Mrs Cummings.'

Steve looks relieved.

They prop O'Donnell against the wall and Fletcher gets his keys out of his pocket.

'What about his pockets?' Steve asks. 'He might have a phone or something.'

This hasn't occurred to Fletcher and, as relieved as he is that Steve has suggested it, he's damned if he's going to give him the credit for it.

'I'm not stupid,' he says, digging around in O'Donnell's suit. 'You think I'd lock him up without checking?'

'No,' says Steve, looking worried. 'Sorry.'

'Just go and check on Mrs Cummings,' Fletcher says. 'I'll be along in a minute.'

Steve jogs back down the corridor and into the transfer room.

Fletcher takes O'Donnell's phone, wallet and keys. He nearly leaves the loose change and then decides that would be a waste. It's not like O'Donnell is likely to ask for it back.

'Every penny goes to a worthy cause,' he says, shoving it all in his own pockets.

Then he opens the door and the foul smell from what's inside washes over him. He shoves O'Donnell's body through the door, rather loving the sound it makes as it lands painfully on the other side, and then he locks the door behind him.

He needs to figure this out. All problems can be solved, all it takes is a bit of thought.

In the room behind him he hears whoever that is inside O'Donnell waking up. There's groaning, swearing, a pause and then a cry of horror. Yeah, thinks Fletcher, don't blame you, I wouldn't want to wake up looking at that either. Why don't the damn things just rot away? Weird aliens. Who needs them?

God, but this is all becoming a mess. This morning he was on top of the world, now he can feel it all falling apart unless he can somehow slam the brakes on. He deserves this, this has been his big break, he's fought for it. There's no way he's going to give it all up now.

15

AN ABATTOIR IN SILHOUETTE

The smell is what wakes him. As Ram struggles to his feet in the dark room he can't even begin to imagine what it is that reeks so badly. His glasses have fallen off, so he puts them back on and squints at the purple, shiny lump in front of him, just barely lit by the light through a dirty window. He finally realises it's a face and the panicked cry that comes from him is entirely involuntary.

In a way, the low light helps him realise what it is he's looking at. If the body parts around him had been clear he might have been distracted by their alienness, but in the semi-darkness, the shape and the foul smell is enough for him to realise he's sitting in the remains of a massacre. They're clearly not human bodies but he can recognise the shape of severed limbs when he's looking at them.

His hands are sticky and he wipes them on the breasts of the suit he's wearing, desperate to be clean. How many bodies are there? He just can't tell, it's an abattoir in silhouette and he's never been more desperate to get out of somewhere in his life.

He gets up and carefully walks over to the window, hoping to get a sense of where he is. The glass is so dirty he can barely see through it, just the vague shape of a wall outside and a thin band of sky above. At least it's not blacked-out like the others. He guesses whoever refitted this place didn't want to come in here, not with all the remains. Maybe that will be useful – could he break the window and get through it before someone comes running? Then he has to remind himself of his new size and wonders if he can get through it at all.

At least he's not dead, though if he's stuck in this body for the rest of his (likely now much shorter) life, he's not entirely sure he wouldn't prefer to be.

So where did all the dead aliens come from? Did Fletcher kill them? Were they already dead when he found this place? Did Fletcher steal all this stuff? It makes sense that it would be alien, it's not like you can pop into the Apple Store and buy body-swap kits, and this obviously isn't an official government set-up.

Who knows? Right now, Ram's not even sure he cares, he just wants to get out. Trapped here, he's in no position to fix anything. At least if he can get free he might be able to do something, to find some way of forcing them to give him his own body back.

In fact, why haven't they swapped him back already? The clue's in the company name, Joyriders; this obviously isn't supposed to be a permanent deal. Whoever's riding around in his body, the owner of this annoying bag of bones is expecting to get his body back. So why hasn't he already? What's gone wrong? They must be hoping to fix it because otherwise he'd be looking like the alien stew he's currently sharing a room with. He's alive because they need him. Is that useful? He thinks it might be. In fact, he thinks he might have the beginnings of a plan. He just hopes this old guy really *does* want his body back. I mean, God knows why, he's currently riding around in perfection. If someone offered to trade you a knackered old Fiat for their Porsche you'd bite their hand off, but surely you wouldn't want to swap back again?

16

DATA RETRIEVAL

John O'Donnell stands in front of the mirror and looks at the beautiful body that will never truly be his.

'You're pretty vain, you know that?' says the boy in the bed.

O'Donnell glances at the reflection of the other body he's borrowed this morning and sneers. 'If I wanted your opinion I'd have paid for that as well.'

The boy shrugs and reaches over to the bedside table for his packet of cigarettes. O'Donnell can't help looking at him, spread out like that, buttocks clenched as he stretches out for his smokes. He feels that borrowed part of him twitch and hates himself for it. If his wife could see him now, his mother, he'd break their hearts.

Not that his mother had much of a heart to break, even before the cancer took her.

'Please,' he says, 'just go.'

The boy now has an unlit cigarette hanging out of his mouth. He stares at O'Donnell's false reflection, scratches his balls and shrugs.

'Suit yourself. It's your time, but you're not getting a refund. You booked me for a couple of hours. I could have got another client.'

Just listen to him, O'Donnell thinks, how easily he sells all that prettiness of his.

'I don't want change,' he says. 'I just want to be on my own.'

The boy starts getting dressed. 'Whatever.'

O'Donnell tries not to watch him while he pulls his clothes on but can't quite tear his eyes away. Finally, the beautiful boy leaves this cheap hotel room and the equally cheap smell of sex left in it.

O'Donnell sits down on the corner of the bed, still staring at this body in the mirror. Part of him wishes he'd never heard of Garry Fletcher. Before him, all of this had just been a fantasy, something he could pretend wasn't real. A phase that had clung to him. (For so many years, John. Can you really call something that's pulsed away inside you for over fifty years a 'phase'?)

To begin with he'd not even believed Fletcher's process was possible of course. Take over someone else's body? Fletcher had admitted that all of his clients were skeptical the first time. But once O'Donnell had accepted what was on offer, he'd convinced himself that it was the perfect opportunity to cure himself of these stupid urges, these dirty urges. He'd put himself in a position where he could act on them, face himself with it, then, for sure, he'd realise he didn't actually want to. Fantasy's one thing but the reality of it? 'Yes,' he'd lied to himself, 'It'll almost be like aversion therapy. I bet you'll never have those thoughts again.'

Ha ha.

Now he barely thought about anything else.

He knew it was wrong, of course he did. They all acted like it was fine these days, men with men, women with women, but he knew better. He'd been brought up properly. His mother had made her feelings quite clear on the subject when she'd caught him kissing Nigel from school. It hadn't meant anything, he'd insisted, they'd just been playing really. But mother knew better. She'd seen it in him, she said, the perversion, the disease. Oh, how she'd hoped she was wrong but deep down, in her heart, she'd known what he was.

She would help him, she promised, cure him.

And he'd tried hadn't he? Certainly he'd tried. He'd stopped looking at boys, got a girlfriend. Poor long-suffering Sandra; she'd always thought there had been something wrong with her, she'd deserved better. He'd never forget her tears and the look on her face, that awful acceptance that whatever was wrong, whatever it was about her that repelled him, she knew it was her fault, knew and hated herself for it. If only he could have found a way to convince her that wasn't true, a way to explain that wouldn't involve him saying that he was... that he might be... that he liked...

Then finally he'd met Cheryl and that was perfect. Cheryl had no interest in the bedroom and had been wildly relieved to find a husband who shared her feelings. With Cheryl the question was never asked, the answer buried deeper and deeper over their years together.

John checks the time on the kid's phone – so many missed calls – did kids spend their whole lives on the damn phone these days? There is still a while left. He gets up and goes to the mirror again, running his fingers over this thing he can never be.

When there is only half an hour left of his allotted time, he showers (only fair, he wouldn't want this body to be contaminated just because of his urges; he feels guilty about that too, not enough to stop him of course, no amount of guilt was enough for that). Then, taking one last regretful look in the mirror ('Maybe I could borrow this body again?') he puts on his clothes and goes downstairs to check out.

He always expects the person at reception to look at him with disgust but they never do. They don't care who you are. They rarely even look at your face. He's prepaid for the room so just hands over the keycard and walks out.

This is always the worst time, walking down the street, knowing that at any moment he is going to end up back in that fat, slow, ugly worthless body of his.

But the moment doesn't come.

He checks the phone again. Fletcher is definitely late. Part of him doesn't mind of course, better to be in this body than his own, but not knowing when the hammer will fall.

Should he call him? Should he see what's going on?

He swipes the phone and taps in the four-digit passcode. Then pauses. How did he know that? This isn't his phone. Does the body remember somehow? An unconscious memory? Have these fingers tapped that number out so many times that they remember it even now, when their owner isn't in possession?

O'Donnell stares at the phone, at the picture of the girl on the home screen. She seems familiar too but that certainly is impossible. There's no way O'Donnell can have met someone this body knew. 'Rachel' he thinks and somehow, impossibly, knows that this is right, that that's this girl's name. He knows something else too: she's dead. Why would you keep the image of a dead girl on your phone? More importantly, how does he know all this?

He's read about how memory is processed, theories that the brain itself can keep a physical store, but this has never happened before, so why now?

For some reason he's still here, and now he's picking up on the host body's memories. Something's wrong. Something's seriously, seriously wrong.

He scrolls through the phone contacts, seeing screen icons and names, and one by one he remembers them all. Then, staring at the picture of a boy called Charlie, he knows something else and, if his mind hadn't already been reeling, it certainly is now.

17

A HARD TIME FOR THE COAL
HILL SCHOOL ADMINISTRATIVE WASTE BIN

'I should have just gone to my ballet lesson,' says the person who on the outside is Amar Sai, an unremarkable Year Eleven student who, until now, has only ever been in trouble for talking in class.

He's sat in the school office, alongside Charlie, April and Tanya. Quill loiters in the doorway as the school counsellor, Toby Moore, does his best to be useful. Mr Moore is beginning to feel a little out of his depth in his current posting. In fact, Mr Moore is giving serious consideration to handing in his notice.

'It just used to be pre-exam nerves and fretting over pubic hair,' he frequently complains to his wife. 'Now the whole place has gone mad and I feel like I'm going mad right along with them.'

To make matters worse, now that the school is stuck in between head teachers he seems to be being allocated a good chunk of the role's duties. To begin with he liked to think it was because the rest of the staff had recognised his abilities and wanted to see them put to good use. Now, a few days in, he realises that he's simply being thrown every job that nobody else wants to deal with. He has become Coal Hill School's Administrative Waste Bin and he feels like he's being buried alive.

'Ballet lesson?' he asks.

Amar nods. 'That's what I usually do, but after last week I started to think about it. Having these lessons is one thing but it's never going to lead to anything is it? It's not like I can actually become a ballet dancer, I just can't. It's a dream, that's all. I'm just getting to pretend on a weekly basis.'

Toby is dreadfully lost. He glances up at Miss Quill, purely because she's the only other source of authority within reach. He doesn't like her very much. In fact being near her often brings out his infrequent stutter.

'We don't do ballet lessons here, do we?' he asks.

'Of course we don't,' she says.

'I didn't think so.'

146

'I don't mean here, you ridiculous man,' says Amar. 'I don't take ballet lessons *here*.'

Ridiculous man? He often feels like one but he's not sure the students should be agreeing with him so openly.

'Please keep your tone civil, Amar,' he says. 'Anger is often useful but we shouldn't direct it at those who are trying to help.' He's slightly proud of this and looks at the other three students, as if expecting them to smile and nod at his well-phrased words. They don't, they're just twitching in their seats seemingly desperate to be anywhere but here. Toby sympathises.

'He doesn't think he's Amar,' says the youngest of the three, Tanya Adeola. 'He says he's called Viola.'

'Like the instrument?' he wonders out loud then wishes he hadn't.

'Oh do shut up,' says Amar. 'You haven't the first idea what you're talking about and I'm wasting my time sat here.'

The boy stands up and moves to leave. Quill makes it quite clear she won't let him. She makes it clear without even moving, something that impresses Toby beyond measure.

'Look,' says Amar drawing to a halt, 'this is nothing to do with you and I haven't paid good money to just sit here being patronised by idiots.'

'He really isn't Amar, is he?' says Charlie, looking at the boy with fascination.

'We should ask where Ram might be,' says April.

Toby is getting even more frustrated by the fact that he seems to be an ignorant spectator to this entire situation.

'Please sit down, Amar,' he says, 'and let's see if we can't get to the bottom of all this.'

'Where's Ram Singh?' April asks.

Amar simply stares at her. 'Never heard of him,' he says. 'Should I have?' He looks up at the clock on the wall and sighs. 'Is that thing right?'

Charlie checks his phone. 'A few minutes slow.'

Amar shrugs. 'It doesn't matter then, my time's almost up anyway.'

'What time?' asks Quill, finally stepping into the room, realising that any slim opportunity this situation offers is vanishing fast.

'The time I've paid for,' says Amar. 'The time I'm stuck here staring at your silly little faces.'

Quill grabs Amar and Toby jumps up out of his chair in shock.

'What are you doing?' he cries.

'Who's behind this?' Quill roars, shaking Amar.

'You can't attack a student!' Toby begs. He knows he should intercede but then Quill might hit him and he's too scared of her to risk that.

'You won't hurt him,' says Amar. 'I know you won't.'

'I won't do any permanent damage, no,' says Quill and pokes her fingers into the pressure points on Amar's arms. He screams. This is too much for Toby, as scared as he is of Quill, he can't just stand here and watch his career go down the toilet.

'Get off him!' he shouts, pulling at Quill.

'He's right, Miss Quill,' says Tanya. 'You can't hurt him, because it *isn't* him is it?'

'I thought you wanted to find your friend,' says Quill, but drops Amar anyway.

'You're a right bitch,' Amar says. 'You know that?'

'Oh yes,' Quill replies with a smile that will give Toby nightmares in the weeks to come.

'Please just tell us where we can find our friend,' begs April.

'Couldn't tell you even if I wanted to,' Amar replies, then his face goes slack for a second before he stares at them in clear confusion.

'What's going on?' he asks.

'It's really him now, isn't it?' says Charlie.

Quill sighs. 'Well, that was a waste of time.'

'At least we know we're right,' says April. She shivers slightly. 'To think that happened to me this morning. It makes me feel sick.'

'Look,' says Toby, 'this has all gone too far now. I haven't the faintest idea what you're all talking about. It's ridiculous and extremely, *extremely* annoying. I demand that everyone leaves the office except for Amar. He and I will have a little chat and, after that…' he looks at Quill, 'I suppose we'll see if you still have a career.'

'Why wouldn't I?' she says and smiles sweetly at Amar. 'Have I ever physically attacked you, Amar?'

Amar is still clearly disorientated but he can answer that question easily enough. 'Of course not.'

'Good boy,' says Quill. 'Don't forget to tell anyone else who asks the same thing.' She looks at the other three. 'Come on, you heard Mr Moore, he needs to have a little sit down and a cry.'

She walks out, Charlie, April and Tanya following behind, somewhat sheepishly.

18
STEVE'S LITTLE PROBLEM

Steve is beginning to think he may be developing an ulcer. Only a few hours ago everything was going so well. He loves this new job, loves the money and loves the infrequent opportunities to finally deal with his Little Problem.

He calls it his Little Problem but nobody else does. Especially his wife who has made it quite clear that he'll never see her or the kids again if she smells a trace of booze on his breath ever again.

Steve is an alcoholic. But that's OK, because now Steve has a job that lets him tie one on at regular intervals without a drop of it ever entering his bloodstream. It's not the perfect solution of course, these mad binges don't stop the constant craving, but knowing that he *can* drink, *will* drink in fact, very soon, just as soon as the boss leaves the office for a bit, makes a hell of a difference. It doesn't deal with the physical cravings but the psychological ones? It helps with those a fair bit. The way he looks at it is this: he can still drink, he just has to binge it. He daren't stay too long in the transfer room – he knows without a doubt that if Fletcher catches him hooked up to the machine he'll be screwed – so he dashes in, transfers over, grabs a bottle he's stashed earlier (the day he spent ten frustrating minutes digging around in a hedge before accepting that some thief had found it and beaten him to it was just the worst), neck it, then feel the buzz for as long as he dare before transferring back to dull sobriety. It isn't perfect, far from it, but just knowing that drink is still available to him, with none of the long-term side effects to his liver or marriage, that's an amazing and beautiful thing.

But it has caused other, small complications. Because although everyone thinks Steve is a bit stupid, he's actually not bad with technology. Even this, weird, alien technology. Which is how he figured out you could set an automatic timing function for transfers, enabling him to run it by himself. It's also why he is now staring at the pyramid and knowing that the reason all hell is breaking loose in the world of Joyriders is that he can't keep his damn hands to himself.

The problem with Mr O'Donnell is Steve's fault. He'd been playing with the controls, exploring functions, seeing what else the thing could do. What he hadn't realised, during his messing about – but did now, oh yes – was that the machine could do a full transfer. That's the only explanation for what's happened. Mr O'Donnell has been sent into the host body and the mind of the host body has been sent into that of Mr O'Donnell. Permanently. Add to that the fact that Steve has been futzing with the timer controls and *boom*, you've got yourself exactly the problem they're facing now. When the timer had gone off, the host mind must have woken up in O'Donnell's body, causing their current problem.

God but he wishes he'd never started tinkering with this thing while Fletcher was out.

God but he wishes he could have a drink.

So how to fix it? How to reverse what he's done? Of course it would help if he could figure out exactly what he *did* do, figure it out precisely, if he can only remember that, then fixing it should be a doddle.

'Time to wake up Mrs Cummings,' says Fletcher, strolling into the room. He doesn't seem to notice the way Steve backs away from the machine, desperately trying to appear like a man who most definitely wasn't just messing about with the controls. Steve is relieved about that.

'Yeah,' he points at the machine, 'do you want me to...?'

'Do me a favour, I'd rather get her back in one piece.' Fletcher pushes him out of the way and Steve watches over his shoulder as he reverses the transfer. He doesn't mind his boss treating him like an idiot, in fact he's relieved by it. If Fletcher believes him incapable of using the machine then he's unlikely to guess what Steve's done.

Mrs Cummings groans slightly and Fletcher dashes over to ensure he's the first thing she sees when she opens her eyes.

'Hello there Mrs Cummings,' he says in the voice Steve knows his boss considers charm itself. Personally, Steve thinks it sounds like a particularly bad waiter in a restaurant that isn't half as posh as it believes it is. Fletcher will insist on being charming with the ladies, even old birds like Mrs Cummings. 'I can have any woman eating out of my hand inside two minutes,' Fletcher frequently claims. Steve has seen precious little evidence of it; they all just look at him as if he's a bit creepy.

'And how was our ballet lesson today?'

Steve notices that she hesitates for a moment, looks awkward.

'Delightful as always, thank you,' she says. 'I'd love to tell you all about it but I have another appointment this afternoon, I'm afraid.'

'Next time,' oozes Fletcher as he leads her out of the door.

The minute they're gone, Steve is back staring at the controls. There must be a way around this, there must be!

He hears Fletcher's phone going off and his boss making apologetic noises to Mrs Cummings as he answers it. Suddenly Fletcher is heading back towards him, talking excitedly on the phone. Steve backs away from the equipment again, grabbing the headset Mrs Cummings has just taken off and making a big show of carefully coiling the cable around his hands as he tidies it up and places it back near the central console.

Fletcher bursts in.

'Steve, my beauty!' he says, and for a moment Steve is terrified, he's never seen this amount of enthusiasm from his boss before and he's quite convinced it can only be a trick, a way of getting him to lower his guard so Fletcher can kill him. He's sure Fletcher killed the last bloke that worked for him, Mike something...

Fletcher doesn't kill him. 'I've solved all our problems. Well, Mr O'Donnell has, to be fair.'

'Really?'

'Yeah, he's only gone and found us the one thing we need to get this machine working properly! He's found us another alien!'

19
NO CONTROL

'We're no better off now than we were already,' Tanya moans. Nobody can disagree with her.

They're heading towards Ram's house because... well, because they have no idea what else to do.

Charlie can't help but notice that April has been quiet.

'Are you alright?' he asks.

'Of course she's not alright,' Tanya interrupts. 'Our friend might be dead in a minute!' Sometimes Charlie is so far away from being human, she thinks, so cold and confused, as if emotions are something he's still working on. He's like a small dog, she thinks, who doesn't bat an eyelid when charging into battle against an Alsatian but would quake in terror at the sight of an unusual stick. It's as if all the responses are there but sometimes he forgets the cues that trigger them.

'It's not that,' April admits, then feels a bit embarrassed. 'Not *only* that anyway, obviously I'm worried for him.'

'What is it then?' asks Charlie.

'Watching the way Amar was. Someone else inside him, someone else in control. That was me this morning. Have you any idea what that feels like?'

'Having another living thing trapped inside your body controlling your actions?' says Quill, who is walking a short distance behind them and has, until this moment, been pretending that she wasn't even listening. 'I can't imagine. Must be horrendous.'

'It's hardly the same thing,' Charlie snaps.

'No, Prince,' Quill replies. 'Of course, Prince, I'm sure it's nowhere near as cruel or invasive as that, Prince.'

At which point she falls silent and resumes pretending she's not with them.

'At least you have control over most of your actions,' April replies. 'I had no control at all. They could have made me do anything. Getting drunk? That was nothing. But I have no idea what else they might have done, no idea at all. And without knowing, I can't help but think the worst, you know? I was completely helpless for, what? Half an hour? A lot can happen in half an hour. One hell of a lot.'

Charlie puts his hand on her shoulder but she flinches so he takes it away again, not knowing what he's supposed to do.

'Sorry,' she says, 'I just ... It's not the first time someone has tried to control me.'

She's thinking of her father. Of that day in the car. Of the roaring engine, the sound of her mother screaming. But she doesn't want to talk about that. Not now. She made a promise to herself after that day. She promised that she would always be in control, that she wouldn't let others dictate her circumstances for her. That promise is going so well right now. Not even her heart is entirely her own.

They've reached Ram's house now, and April's glad to change the subject. 'He's not there, we know he's not there, going in is just going to cause a scene with his dad, you know that, right?'

'I'll go on my own,' says Tanya. 'The rest of you stay out of sight. If Ram's dad is going to kick up a fuss he's not as likely to do it if it's just me.'

Charlie, Quill and April walk off while Tanya heads towards the house.

None of them see the figure watching them from a short distance away.

20

HE JUST MIGHT BE ABLE
TO SAVE THE WORLD

John O'Donnell knows he can't let them see him. If they see him then they'll think he's the boy, their friend, and then questions will be asked and, while he keeps remembering new details, they're sketchy, not enough to let him play the part. Better to stay back, better to watch and remember.

'There,' he thinks, 'posh boy, that's the one. Charlie. That's what it calls itself. That's the name it pretends with. And the woman, the one hanging back from the other two, pretending she's not with them. Not a woman. No. She's like the other one. Wrong. Alien.'

He's surprised by how easily he accepts the idea. It's not because of what he's currently experiencing; the idea of transferring bodies might seem miraculous but he's always imagined it in purely scientific terms. No, the reason he knows those two people aren't what they seem, absolutely *knows* it, is because his host body knows it. He shares its conviction along with everything else. He wonders what other convictions he might end up feeling if he stays in the body too long. What other things will he begin to believe?

So what does he do about it? What does he do about *any* of this?

He needs to call Fletcher, he's decided that much. The initial idea of staying in this body permanently, of maybe even starting a whole new life inside it, has started to sour. Because he'd get caught in the end, he's bound to. Maybe, if all of the boy's memories were opened to him, he might be able to bluff it. Maybe. But he has no guarantee of that. Besides, what if the boy's mind is still in here somewhere? What if that's why he's remembering the few things he has? What if that mind suddenly took control? Where would that leave him?

And there's Cheryl of course, for all he doesn't deserve her, he does love her. He can't just abandon her, their home, their life, his business, everything. However tempting it might be to wipe the slate clean and start a new life in a young and beautiful body, it's just not something he can do. So he needs to change back.

And now there's this. Aliens living amongst them. He's got to do something about that, hasn't he? It could be an invasion! They could want to wipe everyone out. He's lucky he's stumbled on this, it's just possible that his… urges, his crime, might lead to something good after all. He just might be able to save the world!

He calls Fletcher.

21

'I'M GOING TO CUT THIS BLOKE
TO PIECES!'

Steve is finally alone again. Fletcher's excitement doesn't quite make sense to him. Just because he's found an alien – a concept Steve has no problem running with, he's played with this machine too much to balk at that – that doesn't mean they're going to be able to work this thing now does it? What does Fletcher think? That all aliens understand the machinery of all other aliens? That's like assuming all humans know how to split an atom.

Fletcher's enthusiasm wasn't shared by Mrs Cummings either when he begged her to stay a little longer, to help him with 'a little problem'. If she remained he was only too happy to reward her with free transfer time. In fact, he promised her two whole free sessions but she just shook her head and asked to be taken home.

Something had unsettled her during her last transfer, Steve could tell that even if his boss can't. She always makes a big show of being happy, a loud, vivacious figure whenever she visits. She barely talked above a whisper after they revived her. No, something definitely happened. Well, as long as it isn't something that will cause Steve further trouble he doesn't care. For now he has enough things of his own to worry about.

He starts experimenting with the machine, feeling its presence in his head, guiding his fingers, leading him on. What did he do before? What were the precise instructions he gave this damned thing?

From nearby, there's the sound of broken glass and Steve panics so hard he screams and flings himself away from the machine. What now? *What now?!*

He heads out into the corridor in time to hear shouting coming from the room at the end. The room he's not allowed in, on pain of death. The room in which Fletcher locked away the body of Mr O'Donnell.

Why did this have to happen now? Why did it have to happen when Steve was on his own?

'What are you doing in there?' he shouts.

The broken glass. Is there a window in there? Has the body of Mr O'Donnell broken out? Surely Fletcher wouldn't have locked him in a room with a window he could just crawl out of? His boss isn't half as clever as he thinks he is but he's not *that* stupid. Probably.

'Let me out now!' the man shouts from inside the room.

'Good,' Steve thinks, 'he hasn't escaped. That's something at least. Probably just smashed something to kick up a fuss.'

'If you don't let me out,' the man says, 'I'm going to cut this bloke to pieces. I've got broken glass in here and by the time I've finished he won't recognise himself.'

Surely he wouldn't do that? Cut himself up, just to get out?

'Don't think I won't do it!' the voice continues. 'I'm not stupid. As soon as you've done what you need to do, you lot will kill me anyway. So I haven't got anything to lose have I?'

Steve can't believe this. If he could just swap them back then the whole mess would be done with. Everything could go back to normal. Yeah, Fletcher probably wouldn't let the kid live, he knows too much by now, could cause them trouble, but...

'Oh God why do I have to deal with this? It's not fair! It's not fair! IT'S NOT FAIR!'

'Are you listening?' the voice shouts.

'Yeah!' Steve replies, hunting for his phone. 'Just give me a minute.'

'No,' Ram replies, 'you haven't got a minute. I'm serious, unless you open this door right now I am going to start cutting.'

'But I don't have the keys!' Steve replies and, as soon as he's said it he knows that's not actually true. There's a spare set he uses to lock up when Fletcher goes home early. His boss doesn't mind him having them, he thinks he's too scared to go in that room against orders (and normally he'd be right, Steve likes being alive, it's nice).

'Then you'd better figure something out quickly hadn't you? Because if I cut too deeply this bloke's going to be dead and then what are you going to do, eh?'

Then the voice screams and Steve can just imagine the broken glass cutting into Mr O'Donnell and it's just the very worst thing and…

'Wait! Wait! I'm coming!'

So how does he do this? Maybe he can convince the kid in O'Donnell's body that he can transfer him back. And maybe he can! Given a bit of time maybe he can actually pull that off. Yes! And then, when Fletcher gets back, he'll have solved the problem and he won't need this alien he thinks he's found after all. He might even give Steve a raise!

'Two secs,' he shouts, 'the keys are in the desk!'

He runs into the foyer, opens a drawer in the desk and pulls out the set of keys.

'Don't cut him!' he shouts, running down the corridor, trying to figure out which key it must be by process of elimination.

He tries one in the lock, it doesn't work. 'I'm doing it,' he shouts, 'just finding the right key. Please don't cut him again!' The second key he tries works and he opens the door.

'Oh please,' says Ram as he punches Steve in the face as hard as he possibly can, 'I faked cutting him the first time. I'm not that stupid.'

Ram punches Steve a few times, hoping that repetition is as good as skill or strength, then grabs the keys out of the moaning man's hands and sprints for the front door. He heard the other guy leave earlier, and he's pretty sure there's nobody else here but he keeps on his toes anyway, staying tense just in case someone suddenly appears. Nobody does.

He's straight out of the front door and out into fresh air, finally!

He keeps going, running down a small access road and then out into a main street, he spins around, sees a sign. Swallow Avenue. He doesn't know where it is, so he keeps running, making for the end of the road, sure he'll recognise something if he can just—

He comes juddering to a halt, a stitch blazing away in his side.

'Oh God,' he says, pushing his glasses back up his nose from where they've slipped down. 'Fat Man just isn't built for running.'

He gets his breath for a minute, trying to figure out what to do next.

He checks his pockets on the off chance he has anything useful, not knowing Fletcher cleaned them out earlier. He finds a receipt for a hotel booking but nothing else. He needs to find a phone. He can remember Tanya's number. If he can find a phone he can call her, but will she believe him? He doesn't sound like himself. Can he convince her? He thinks for a minute and knows he can. What with everything that's happened to them lately it's easy enough to prove he is who he says he is.

Then what? Somehow, he has to get back in that room with all the equipment and force them to change him back. But what if Joyriders does a runner once the boss knows Ram's escaped? Could they do that? Just clear off? If they can then he's really screwed. It's been hard enough accepting he's lost some of his skills at football, there's no way he's spending the rest of his life in a body that can't even run a couple of hundred metres without being five minutes from death.

He needs to stay close to Swallow Avenue, quickly get hold of Tanya, tell her where he is, get her to rustle up as many of them as she can and then meet him back here. Yes. This is a plan that works.

So were to find a phone?

He walks along the street a bit further, trying to see where it leads. Maybe he'll come out on a main road, somewhere that might have a callbox or something. Do they even have callboxes any more? Ram is not someone who has ever had to worry about not having a phone. The idea of being so cut off from others is frustrating as hell.

On the other side of the road a woman is walking along with a young child. Maybe he can borrow her phone? She glances at him, sees he's looking at her and then grabs her child closer and speeds up. Why's she being like that? Why is she acting like she's scared of him? Then he looks down at himself, suit dishevelled, covered in gross alien gunk. Who wouldn't think he was trouble?

He tries to tidy himself a bit.

At the end of Swallow Avenue, he looks each way and decides his chances are better to the right: he can hear traffic and the distant hiss of hydraulic bus brakes.

He keeps walking and eventually finds himself on Old Street. Now he's getting somewhere!

Even better, just up the road he can see a couple of call boxes.

He jogs along, waiting to be able to cross and then dashes over to the closest box.

Climbing inside – Christ, it's even hard to do that wearing Fat Guy, he's never realised how small these things are before – he suddenly notices he hasn't got any change for the call.

Reverse charges? Is that still a thing? He scans through the instructions on the phone, trying to figure out how you'd call the operator. He finds it, picks up the phone and dials.

'Hello, operator speaking.'

'Yeah, hi. I need a reverse charge call please.'

'Can you give me the number?'

'Yeah, of course, it's 079—'

The operator interrupts him. 'I'm sorry, collect calls are only available to UK fixed lines, not mobiles.'

Ram's frustration suddenly bursts and he swears loud enough for people on the pavement to turn and look.

'There's no need for language like that.'

Ram panics, not wanting the operator to hang up. 'Sorry, sorry, it's been a bit of day. Look, this is an emergency.'

'I can connect you to emergency services, which service do you require?'

'No, that's OK, I need to speak to this person specifically.'

'Do you have the fixed line of the person you're trying to call?'

Ram thinks. 'No, I … Wait, can you look it up?'

'If they're directory listed.'

'Great!' Now he might be getting somewhere. 'It's Tanya Adeola… No, it won't be listed under her name. Hang on…' What's her mum's name? Think Ram, think! 'Vivian!'

'No need to shout, sir.'

'Sorry, sorry.'

'That's Vivian Adeola?'

'Yes.'

'And the address?'

'Oh…' He doesn't know that. He's trying to think of it anyway, as if he might be able to just guess. 'I'm not sure. It's Shoreditch area.'

'So, an E1 postcode?'

'I guess so, probably. Is that enough?'

'I'm really supposed to get a full address.'

'Oh please! This is honestly an emergency, I really need to get hold of her.'

There's silence. Ram is trying to decide what the pause means. Is the operator considering whether to tell him? Are they already looking? Have they hung up?

'There's only one V. Adeola listed in the E1 area,' the voice says eventually. 'Putting you through now. Your name?'

'Ram Singh.'

'Thank you Mr Singh.'

The phone rings. And rings. Then it rings once more.

'Hello?' It's a male voice. Who's that, Ram wonders?

'I have a collect call from Ram Singh, will you accept the charges?'

'Ram what now?' says the voice.

'Just say yes!' Ram shouts.

'A Ram Singh, calling for a Tanya Adeola?'

'Oh,' the voice says. 'Yeah, OK, whatever…'

'Carry on Mr Singh,' says the operator, and then, with an unexpected warmth, 'hope she's worth it.'

Ram has no idea what to say to that and is relieved to hear the operator disconnect.

'Hi,' he says, 'is Tanya there?'

'No,' says the voice. 'This is Damon, her brother. Her *older* brother.'

Why's he putting emphasis on the older part? Ram wonders, does he think… ? Oh God, he thinks I'm a boyfriend.

'I'm not a boyfriend!' he blurts out.

'Good, you sound like you're forty or something.'

'I'm just a friend, from school, but I really need to speak to her.'

'Call her mobile then.'

'I tried that, I've…' He decides to tell as much of the truth as Damon will believe, 'Someone's stolen all my cash, my phone, everything.'

'Yeah? That sucks.'

'Yeah, so I had to do, like, a reverse charge thing but you can't do that to mobiles apparently so—'

'So here you are.'

'Yeah.'

'But she ain't here.'

'I know, I know! But look, is there any way you can get a message to her? I wouldn't ask but it's really important.'

'What message?'

'Tell her I'm on Swallow Avenue.'

'Like the bird.'

In the background Ram can hear the sound of a games console, and Damon calls back over his shoulder to someone else in the room. 'I'm trying to talk to someone here.'

'Swallow Avenue,' says Ram, 'you got that? It's just off Old Street.'

'OK. What about it?'

'Just tell her that's where I am. Tell her to bring everyone, I'll meet them there.'

'This something I need to tell Mum about?'

'How old are you Damon?'

Damon laughs. 'Point. OK, I'll call her.'

'Thanks, you're a star.'

Ram hangs up. OK. That's good. They know where he is (as long as Damon *does* call her of course). He squashes that thought straight away – of *course* he'll call her. He said he would, so why wouldn't he?

Ram steps out of the phone box and crosses the road. Now all he has to do is hang around Swallow Avenue and wait, keeping an eye on the Joyriders place. Once they're all together then they'll think of what to do next. There must be a way they can force them to swap him back.

He cuts off Old Street, heading back towards Swallow Avenue.

The problem with all this stuff they keep getting caught up in, he decides, is that they can never go to the authorities about it. If you think about what he's been through, everything that's happened, Poppy and Max... Obviously nobody would believe them, so, because it's so crazy he has to put up with walking around looking like this. Stupid, isn't it? He should just be able to walk in somewhere, explain what's happened and someone will sort it out. He just wants to play football, get through school; why should he be having to watch out for all this as well?

He checks over his shoulder before crossing the road and finds himself staring right at Fletcher. The man's sat behind the wheel of the car, slowed to a crawl in the middle of the road, staring right back at him.

Oh to hell with it all.

Ram runs, as fast as these old legs will carry him. He should have been more careful! To have got away only to end up wandering along, head miles away and have the sod right on his tail again.

Fletcher accelerates, and, obviously, there's no way Ram is going to outrun a car.

But he tries.

22

LYING LIKE A TRUE ADULT

'Ram's dad still hasn't heard from him,' says Tanya, walking away from Ram's house and back to her friends. 'I tried to make it seem like there wasn't anything to worry about.'

'Why would you do that?' Charlie asks.

'Because he was upset and it doesn't help,' explains Tanya. 'If something does happen to Ram then…' she shrugs, 'it does. But until then what's the point in his dad panicking? It's not like he can help.'

'What did you tell him then?' asks April.

'The truth, in a way. I said that Ram has been suffering a lot since Rachel and that he didn't like people fussing about him. That he probably just needed to be on his own for a bit. I said he'd probably turn up later and that, for now, the best thing to do was just to give him some space.'

'You lie like a true adult,' says Quill and they start walking again, heading back to her and Charlie's house.

'He also asked whether there were still weird things going at the school,' Tanya says. She smiles. 'I lied about that too.'

'So, now what do we do?' asks April.

'Is there anything we *can* do?' says Charlie. 'If there's no way of finding Ram, or tracing where the people that are doing this are, then I don't see what options we have.'

Back at Charlie's house, Matteusz is waiting outside.

'I do not like that look,' he says, watching the group walking towards him. 'You all have it. It is a look that says we are doing something weird again.'

'Your boyfriend's clever, Charles,' says Quill, pushing Matteusz out of the way so that she can unlock the door. 'I wonder what he sees in you?'

They all file in, Charlie, April and Tanya explaining to Matteusz what's been happening or, at the very least, what they *think* has been happening. Charlie boils the kettle and they miserably settle down in the front room. Quill can no more bear the thought of staying in the same room as them than she can imagine digging out her eyes with a plastic spoon, so she goes to hide on the small balcony where she can pretend to be picking off passers-by with a sniper rifle. Occasionally she glances through the window and sneers at them, sitting together and chatting over cups of tea. How human, how pointless.

'So we're just going to sit here?' April asks, staring into her mug and wondering how precisely it's going to help.

'I don't know what we're supposed to do,' Charlie replies. 'I suppose we could just walk everywhere, see if we can find him, but how likely is it? At least here we're all together.'

'So we can keep an eye on each other,' agrees Tanya.

The fact that this could happen to her again hasn't occurred to April. The thought of it makes her shake so much she has to put her mug down.

'I'm going to try and call him again,' says Tanya, pulling her phone out of her pocket.

'Tanya,' says April, 'you've tried him, I don't know, every half an hour or something. He's not answering.'

'Doesn't hurt to... Oh God! Missed calls!' Tanya starts tapping at her phone in a panic. 'I knocked the ringer off by accident, he's probably been trying to...' She sees who's been calling, 'Forget it, it's just home.' Never has hope been sucked from a room so quickly.

'You'd better call them,' says Charlie, 'you can say you're staying here if you like.'

'Tell your mum you're staying with me, not Charlie,' says April.

'I know!' says Tanya, as if it's obvious.

'Why?' asks Charlie.

'Because you are a boy, stupid,' laughs Matteusz. 'Not the sort of boy Tanya's mum has to worry about but…'

Tanya waves her hand in the air, trying to get everyone to shut up.

'Hello,' she says, assuming it's going to be her mum who answers. 'I'm over at April's at the moment, sorry, should have—'

'Oh shut up,' says her brother. 'It's Damon. I've tried to call you like a hundred times.'

'Why are you calling me?'

'I can't call you?'

'You know what I mean!'

'Some guy rang the house. Did a reverse charge thing for the phone so I'm going to get an earful over that when mum sees the bill.'

'What guy?'

'Someone called Ram?'

Tanya nearly drops the phone. 'Ram called you? Why did he call you?'

Everyone in the room is now staring at her, desperately waiting for more information. Even Quill stops her imaginary take-down of the entire street and pays closer attention through the window.

'He didn't call me, he called the flat. I think he tried you on your mobile, or couldn't… Anyway it doesn't matter, he says he's at some place called Swallow Avenue. You know it?'

'Swallow Avenue? No, never heard of it. What's he doing there?'

'How do I know? He just told me to tell you. So I'm telling you.'

'That's all he said?'

'He said you should bring everyone. Whoever 'everyone' might be.'

'Oh.'

'Tanya?'

'Yeah?'

'How old is this Ram?'

'How old? Seventeen, why?'

'Really? Weird. He sounded old. Whatever. He asked me to tell you and I have. You coming back late? Want me to tell Mum you're at April's?'

'Yeah, please.'

'OK, don't make me regret it though.'

'I won't, got to go.'

She hangs up. 'That was Damon. Ram called.'

'We know!' April cries. 'So what's going on?'

'He says he's somewhere called…'

Tanya's face suddenly becomes vague, her words petering out.

'What's wrong?' asks Charlie. 'You don't look…'

Tanya smiles and Charlie knows instantly that he's not really looking at his friend. Tanya would never smile like that. It's the smile of someone who's just spotted a fly they can pull the legs off.

'Good times roll!' she shouts, which makes no sense to Charlie whatsoever.

She looks at him, eyeing him up, making a decision. 'Confused? Dopey look? Yeah, I guess you're the kid we're after! We'd like to talk to you.'

Charlie looks to Matteusz, only to see he's looking distinctly uncomfortable. 'Yes,' Matteusz says, with no trace of his normal accent. 'Sorry but we need to, erm, borrow you for a bit.'

'Don't say no,' April adds, leaning in, 'or we'll slap you all the way back to Mars.'

23
NOBODY TELLS GARRY FLETCHER WHAT TO DO

Fletcher is relieved that Mrs Cummings is happy to be dropped off at the Barbican. Today is just grating at him from all sides and the last thing he needs is to be stuck in traffic playing nursemaid to her. At least she's not talking about her dancing like usual. Fletcher only really enjoys dancing that involves vertical poles.

The very minute he gets her out of the car his phone rings. He glances at it, it's from the same number O'Donnell was using. He answers.

'Mr O'Donnell? I just need twenty minutes, I had to drop off another client.'

'This is more important than your little business, Fletcher!' O'Donnell says. It's so weird hearing him talk in that kid's voice. 'We could be dealing with an invasion here!'

'Well, from what you said it's just one kid and a woman so I don't think…'

'It doesn't matter what they look like, Fletcher, or has your entire livelihood escaped you? They could be disguised, they could have taken over human bodies!'

Fletcher supposes he has a point there.

'OK, well, like I say I'll be back in the transfer room shortly and I'll pick them up.'

'Excellent, then we can contact the proper authorities.'

'Well, let's not be silly Mr O'Donnell. There's no need to call anyone official in just yet, is there?'

Fletcher has no intention of doing anything of the kind. He's on a recruitment drive, not a witch hunt. He wants these aliens to help him deal with the machinery, that's all.

'What else are we supposed to do?' O'Donnell asks. 'This could be a matter of… of…' he's struggling to think of the right words, '*planetary* security. What if there are more of them? We need to deal with this properly. I have no idea what agency would deal with something like this – MI6? Special Branch?'

Fletcher's nerves are getting shorter by the second. He's got enough on his plate without this overblown idiot causing even more problems. Why is today being such a bitch? It's getting so he can barely think straight. If only he could have ten minutes just to clear his head, just to come up with some kind of plan.

'Here's an idea,' he says. 'I'll control them, have them walk in somewhere anonymously and admit everything. That way we don't have to be directly involved.'

'But will anyone believe them?'

'Will anyone believe *us*? I'm sure we can figure it out. There's got to be a way of doing this without all of us getting it in the neck as well.'

O'Donnell thinks about this. 'No, it's too important. I think I should call someone now.'

'Please Mr O'Donnell!' Fletcher shouts, seriously close to losing the thin shred of patience he has left. 'There's no need for that, we'll deal with this. Let's just meet up first, talk it through.'

'You won't change my mind, Fletcher. But very well, I've sent you a text message of the house address.'

'Great, I'll be right there.'

Fletcher hangs up, shaking. He's had enough of this. This morning he was running a lovely little business, bringing in a lot of coin, now he's being pulled in all directions with one problem after another. He just can't be doing with it. Time to take some serious action. 'He'll be right there?' No chance. But *someone* will and that will be the end of the annoying Mr O'Donnell. He should have just killed him earlier, he should have known the old man would be trouble. But no, he had to let greed get in the way.

It reminds him of Mike, of how, after only a couple of weeks, he had already been insisting what they should do. Like it was his damn business or something.

'We could do anything with this!' Mike had insisted. 'It doesn't just have to be joyrides for the rich, we could make some serious, big changes to the world. We could take on terrorists! You're thinking too small.'

Obviously, that was a conversation that was going to go nowhere and Fletcher had made good use of the machine that night. A very excitable client had described the look on Mike's face when, with a violent flick of hair braids and a crooked smile, the teenage girl standing next to him on the Tube platform had shoved him into the path of a train at Edgware Road. One satisfied customer and the problem of Mike solved, if only business could always be that simple.

There was one thing that Fletcher simply couldn't stand: people telling him what to do.

Now, with Mike gone, he made do with Steve, stupid, greedy Steve. What he lacked in common sense he made up for with a lack of ambition. With a bit of luck he might get to keep this member of staff for the foreseeable future. If there still was one after today.

He punches the dashboard, his stomach still churning with anger.

He turns the car off Old Street and immediately rethinks Steve's career prospects. Right in front of him is the body of that fat bastard who is trying to ruin his business. 'Well now,' thinks Fletcher, 'this is what we businessmen call an opportunity.'

He doesn't think about it, he just acts. He stamps down on the accelerator and charges towards the now running O'Donnell. 'Go straight on,' he mutters, 'go straight on.' Because if the kid in O'Donnell's body turns left down Swallow Avenue there'll be witnesses. If he keeps going straight he'll find himself in a narrow back road, a road with a high wall on one side and a row of garage lock-ups on the other. A road that has good odds on being empty, a road where something really useful might happen.

The kid goes straight on.

Following the curve of the road, Fletcher slows down again. He waits until he can check all is clear. He glances at the mirror. There's nobody in sight, just him and the body of this fat old pain in the arse.

The kid stops, flailing around in the middle of the road.

'Out of breath?' Fletcher asks, chuckling to himself as he guns the accelerator again.

He makes eye contact with his target, smiling at the look of panic and confusion on that stupid face. Fletcher tenses as the car hits O'Donnell's body. It bounces right over the roof, coming to land on the road behind. That's probably enough, Fletcher thinks, but he's not a man to take risks, so, checking through the windows again, he stops, slips the car into reverse and makes doubly sure. He actually rolls over O'Donnell, bouncing so much in his seat that he bangs the top of his head on the car roof.

'For God's sake,' he rubs at his sore head, this man really is causing him grief today. He's so angry that he's tempted to drive forward and go for one more sweep, just out of spite. There's no need though, he can see that. O'Donnell's body is twisted in an ugly way, legs splayed in the wrong direction to the knee joint, arms twisted and sticking up like tent spikes.

Well, that's one problem dealt with. He'll probably have to ditch the car as soon as possible, depends how bad he's dented the front, but that's no big deal. He'll get Steve to drive it somewhere and dump it later. No, not Steve, because Steve has clearly proven how reliable he is.

Fletcher drives back towards the courtyard, ready to do some serious shouting. Then he suddenly remembers he needs to pick up two afternoon clients and he's already running late. With everything else it has slipped his mind.

This is the last straw on his temper. For a second he just roars, pounding out his anger on the steering wheel. He's surrounded by problems, he feels like the whole damn world is trying to get in the way and he's had enough. Being Garry Fletcher is supposed to be brilliant. He's not supposed to have to deal with all these issues.

He calms down, takes a few deep breaths and then reverses back onto the main road and towards Old Street station. Luckily he's only a few minutes away, these are two of his original clients and he trusts them enough to let them make their own way as far as Shoreditch. If this was someone new on the list he could easily have an hour of driving to contend with, but hopefully he'll be back within a quarter of an hour.

He can get them hooked up and enjoying themselves and then he can deal with the alien kid. Except he can't can he? Someone has to operate the machine. The anger starts rising again. OK, so he'll have to let Steve transfer. He'll operate the machine, Steve can take over the alien kid and… But what about the other one? The adult? The machine won't work on an adult over that distance. How is he supposed to control her?

Oh Christ. What a mess.

OK, wait, how about this? He'd considered it earlier with Mrs Cummings but she'd been too distracted to even listen. He'll offer his clients a special deal. They help him out with a small favour, bringing the kid and the woman here (if they go in mob-handed they should be able to deal with one woman, surely?). Then, once he's got the aliens safely under his control, he'll let his clients have a couple of free transfers by way of payment. Yeah. That might work. He doesn't have to tell the clients what's going on, he can spin them any old toss. Yeah! This'll work. Give it a couple of hours and he'll be back on track.

The sound of his boss returning sets Steve into a panic. He's all ready to explain what's happened, he's sure he can make Fletcher see that, actually, if they just think about it for a minute, it's all going to be OK.

He runs to the reception only to see his boss leading in their next two clients. Should he talk about it in front of them? Probably not. The look on Fletcher's face tells him all he needs to know about the sort of mood he's in.

'I've dealt with our little problem regarding Mr O'Donnell,' Fletcher says and Steve goes cold. 'So count yourself lucky. Also,' he removes the blindfolds from the clients, 'thanks to the kind generosity of Mr Banks and

Mr Taylor here, we'll soon have the expert assistance we've been hoping for.'

'We're going on a mission!' says Banks, offering the sort of spittle-heavy laugh that always makes Steve squint. That involuntary eye twitch you get from standing next to someone who's hammering in a nail.

'Yeah!' says Taylor, 'An extra half-hour's jolly off the books!'

'Expert assistance?' Steve asks, somewhat confused.

'The unusual people Mr O'Donnell located for us earlier,' says Fletcher, giving him a narrow look, a look that says, as clearly as if it were written in neon, 'keep your mouth shut'.

'Unusual people?' Steve thinks. But if Fletcher's dealt with O'Donnell then they don't *need* the aliens any more do they? He tries to think how best to phrase this without saying too much.

'Are you sure we still need to, erm, discuss our running requirements with them Mr Fletcher?' he asks 'After all, if the situation with Mr O'Donnell is dealt with—'

'Just leave the thinking to me,' says Fletcher, patting Banks on the arm in a way he hopes will convey the jocular mood of a man who knows what's what. 'I know what I'm doing.'

'But you don't,' thinks Steve. 'You so clearly don't.'

'Let's get you two hooked up,' Fletcher says, leading Banks and Taylor down the corridor.

Steve dislikes these two. They're exactly the sort of corporate types he thinks the world would be better off without. All posh suits and loud voices, a portfolio where their soul should be.

'If you're sure, Mr Fletcher,' he says. He just can't think of a way of discussing what's happened with his boss without giving the game away. Still, he supposes he'll have a chance once the clients are hooked up. He'll be able to talk freely then and hopefully, between them, they can get all this ironed out.

But that's not going to happen, as is made clear to him a few minutes later.

'You want me to go as well?' he asks, absolutely terrified.

'Don't worry old cock,' says Banks, 'we'll hold your hand if you're worried.'

Fletcher is scowling at the map presented on the machine.

'Looks like there are four viable transfers at that address but one of them keeps flickering in and out. What's all that about then?'

Steve tries to be subtle again. 'Maybe the "expert" isn't entirely compatible with the machine?' he suggests.

Something about the alien's physiology must be clashing with the sensors.

Fletcher stares at him, clearly surprised. Then covers it up. '*Obviously*, that was my whole point, so you'll have to transfer to the other three and, well…' he grins, 'be really convincing! Just get them over here, whatever it takes.'

'This is so wrong,' Steve thinks, but has no idea how to fix it.

'Come on,' says Taylor, leading him over to one of the benches. 'Trust me, you'll love it!'

Steve sits down, considers arguing one more time, then looks at Fletcher's face and realises there simply isn't any point. He puts the headset on and lies back.

Banks gives a whoop of joy and puts on his own headset.

'Come on then lads, let the—'

And they're gone.

24

'I REALLY DON'T WANT YOU KILLING MY FRIENDS.'

Charlie does his best to get out of the way of the three people who are clearly no longer his friends. He's known them such a short time but the difference in them is profound. Tanya's energy has become a simmering threat of violence, April's gentility is now all nervous twitches and clutching fingers, Matteusz's grace is lost to awkward movements, the sign of someone who doesn't know how to move without accidentally breaking something.

'You want to borrow me?' he asks. 'I don't know what you're talking about.'

'I say we slap him anyway,' says April. 'Partly for fun, yeah? But also just to show we mean business.'

'I'm up for that,' says Tanya. 'Fletcher didn't say we couldn't enjoy ourselves, did he?'

'There's no need,' Matteusz insists. He looks pleadingly at Charlie. 'Please just come with us. It'll be much easier if you do.'

'Screw easy,' says April, leaping on Charlie with an enthusiastic roar. 'I vote complicated but fun!'

'Yeah!' cries Tanya, joining in, the pair of them pulling Charlie to the ground and laughing.

The door from the balcony crashes open and Quill moves in, grabbing both April and Tanya by the hair and yanking them back off Charlie.

'Ow, you bitch!' says April, holding onto her head.

'Yeah, having long hair kind of hurts,' adds Tanya.

'As much as I, obviously, approve of anyone wanting to punch Charles, I'm afraid I'm not permitted to allow it,' says Quill. 'Anyone wanting to lay a finger on him has to go through me.'

'OK,' says April, running towards Quill with a laugh.

'No!' Charlie shouts, but not quick enough to stop Quill punching April and sending her sprawling across the floor.

'Don't hurt them, Quill,' he says. 'You can't.'

'Can't not,' Quill replies. 'Remember? If they try to physically harm you I have to stop them.' She taps at her head. 'If you don't like it, maybe you should have thought twice about having this thing put in my head.'

'Please just come with us,' begs Matteusz.

'Don't see why we should,' Quill replies. 'Do you?'

'Because someone's going to get hurt otherwise.'

'Jesus, that guy's a pussy,' says Tanya.

'I know,' April agrees, holding a hand to her sore face. 'I wish he'd stayed back there to work the machine, at least Fletcher's got a spine.'

'So have you, I'm sure,' says Quill. 'And if you attack the boy again I'll pull it out of you and beat your friend to death with it.'

'I like her!' says Tanya. 'She's hot!'

'Yes,' says Quill with a sigh. 'Well, that's going to go down as one of the most unpleasant moments of my life. The time Tanya Adeola lusted after me.'

'It's not Tanya,' says Charlie.

'I'm aware of that,' Quill rolls her eyes. 'I was just… Oh never mind.'

'We should run,' Charlie says.

'Why?' Quill is incredulous. 'They're no threat to me.'

'But you are to them, and I really don't want you killing my friends.'

'This is stupid,' says April storming out and heading for the kitchen. 'It was supposed to be fun, not about getting punched in the face.'

Tanya sidles over to one of the bookshelves, picks up a decorative paperweight, tosses it up and down in her hand like a ball for a few seconds, and then throws it at Quill. Quill steps aside, with no discernible effort.

'If you're going to start destroying the knick-knacks,' she says, 'may I suggest you start with the candlesticks by the television? They're particularly grotesque and I've been meaning to smash them to pieces myself. Quite why your species likes to surround itself with pointless clutter I'll never know.'

'Bitch, you talk too much,' says April, walking back in. She has a large knife in her hand. 'Maybe we should shut you up, yeah?'

'We can't kill them!' says Matteusz. 'You know we can't!'

'Christ,' April sighs. 'You want to keep your mouth shut? Maybe I'll kill you instead.'

She looks at Quill. 'So? You still want to fight me?'

'Well,' says Quill. 'You have a knife so you're presenting a clear threat to the life of my charge.'

'What?' April sneers.

Quill moves faster than April can even react. From her perspective there's just a blur of movement and then a blinding pain in her neck. Then she doesn't know anything at all.

Tanya stares at Quill, who is now holding the knife. April has fallen to the floor, unconscious.

'That was genuinely cool,' Tanya says.

'So glad you enjoyed it,' Quill says. 'Here…'

She tosses the knife, handle first, Tanya grabs it. She looks down at it. 'Why are you giving me this?' she asks, looking up just in time to see Quill fill her vision. Then, for James Banks, property developer and current occupant of Tanya Adeola, the world goes away for a bit.

Quill looks at Matteusz. 'Want to try?'

'No!' he cries. 'God no!'

Charlie, panicking, is checking April. 'You'd better not have harmed her,' he says.

'Well, I've harmed her a *bit*, obviously, she's unconscious. But she'll recover.' Quill grabs him by the arm and drags him towards the front door. 'Shall we go?'

'We're just going to leave them there?' he asks.

'I think that's best, don't you? The next time they try and harm you I may do some permanent damage.'

She pulls him outside. 'And it's not as if we don't know where we're going.'

'Swallow Avenue?'

'You were paying attention after all, good.'

Charlie pulls his arm free of hers and straightens his clothes. 'You enjoyed that, didn't you?'

'What? You think I'm so petty as to have taken pleasure in finally being able to knock around some people who have been less than appreciative of me?'

'Yes, I do.'

'Then you're not as stupid as I thought,' Quill smiles. 'Good for you. Now, where is this Swallow Avenue?'

'I haven't a clue. How would I know?'

Quill sighs, 'I thought it was somewhere you were familiar with.'

'No,' Charlie takes out his phone. 'I'm sure we can find it with this, though.' He opens the map application and taps in the address. 'It doesn't look far. Ten minutes' walk maybe?'

'Fine.'

'And what do you plan on doing when we get there?'

'Oh, I imagine it'll involve beating someone up.'

25

STEVE TRIES TO COME UP
WITH A PLAN

Steve really doesn't know what he's supposed to do. He looks at the unconscious bodies of the two girls and seriously considers just running as far and as fast as he possibly can. Thing is, what's the point? As soon as he's pulled out of this body he'll be face-to-face with Fletcher again anyway.

He pats his pockets and finds Matteusz's phone. He tries to remember Fletcher's number and realises he can't. What's the point of phone contacts if you have to remember everyone's number? He puts the phone away again. Should he maybe follow the other two? Is that a good idea? Might that spare him from a sound beating? (If only he thought that was the worst thing that might happen. He's under no illusions that Fletcher wouldn't happily kill him. No illusions at all.)

One of the girls, the black one, starts groaning. Which one is that? Banks or Taylor? Not that he favours either. They're both as awful as each other.

Maybe it would be better if he weren't around when they woke up? They didn't seem very pleased with him, after all. In fact they might decide to take out their frustration on him. Could they kill him? For one panicked moment he's not sure, then he gets his head together. No, of course not, the whole point is that he's effectively invulnerable in this body. They can hurt him but they can't kill him. Good, that's one thing then.

Except, he really doesn't fancy being hurt either.

No, the best plan is to run away now, follow the two aliens, then, when he does have to face Fletcher he can at least make a sound case for having *tried* to be useful. It's not as if anybody would expect him to be able to kidnap two people on his own, is it? Especially given the punchy one, the really scary, ninja woman from hell. Banks and Taylor will certainly back him up on that.

So, yes, good, he's finally made a decision. He finally has a workable plan. Run away. He heads towards the door.

'Where do you think you're going?' asks whichever of the horrible people is in the white girl.

'Following them, obviously!' he says, trying to sound as if this is the sort of answer that nobody in their right mind could argue with, the sort of answer that can only have all sensible people nodding and waving him on his way.

'Yeah,' says the man who isn't April. 'Fair enough, we'll come with you. You alright, Banksy?'

'Yeah,' says the man who isn't Tanya, getting to his feet. 'Let's get those bastards.'

Steve doesn't like his plan any more.

Taylor tucks the knife into the back pocket of April's jeans and pulls the hem of her T-shirt down over it. 'You see that?' he asks, turning around.

'No,' says Banks. 'You're fine.'

'Great,' Taylor pushes Steve towards the door, 'Come on then.'

26

WARRING IN SUBURBIA

Quill moves so quickly that Charlie is forced into an awkward half-jog just to keep up. The main thing that irritates him about this is that he knows she's doing it on purpose.

'If we're going to wherever it is these people operate from,' he says, 'we could have just agreed to let them take us.'

'Yes, we could. But then we would have been there under their control and, present company excepted, *naturally*, I don't believe in being under someone else's control. Besides, we don't know if Swallow Avenue *is* where they're operating from, do we?'

'I can't see why Ram would be asking us to go there otherwise.'

'I imagine it's probably a trap.'

Charlie rolls his eyes. 'You would think that.'

'It is precisely because I always assume the worst, young man, that you are still alive.'

Charlie can't be bothered to argue as he knows he's bound to lose.

'But we're still going?'

'We've spent the entire day getting absolutely nowhere purely because we didn't know what to do or where to go. After a couple of hours of that, I'll happily take a trap over more sitting around.'

'No wonder you ended up getting caught,' he mutters.

Quill suddenly stops. 'I beg your pardon?'

Charlie realises he's probably gone too far but is too annoyed with her to back down. 'Well, with that sort of attitude, it's surprising you and the revolution survived for as long as you did, isn't it?'

'You're pushing your luck, Prince.'

'Why? What are you going to do? Hit me? You can't, remember?'

Quill turns and carries on walking. 'No, but I could just go home, couldn't I?'

'No, because I'm going to Swallow Avenue whether you want to or not, and as long as I might be in danger you have to look after me.'

Quill roars with frustration. Several people on the street turn in panic to look at them. 'And that is why you are just as bad as the people who are doing whatever this is,' she says. 'You hide behind false principles and smug superiority but your people took me and turned me into a puppet.'

'It was punishment for what you did!'

'It was a way of getting the best bodyguard in the world at a price only one person would regret paying – *me*. Loyalty is something you have to earn, damn you. I spent my whole life earning it; I risked my life earning it. How do you get it? By putting a permanent gun to my head. I tell you, anyone, *anyone* who goes to those measures to achieve loyalty doesn't deserve any in the first place.'

Charlie is genuinely thrown. 'I've never asked for your loyalty,' he says.

'Of course not. You don't have to. If I don't give it automatically, half of my frontal lobe will end up running out of my nose. Which way now?'

He doesn't quite follow that she's changed the subject for a moment. Then checks the map app on his phone and points over the road. 'Up there.'

She storms off in the direction he's pointed, forcing him to jog to catch up again.

'You say it like you don't deserve what happened to you,' he says, finding it hard to walk and talk at this speed. 'Don't forget how many of my people you killed.'

'I won't,' she says. 'I relished each and every one of them.'

This stops Charlie in his tracks. 'You don't mean that.'

Quill stops too. No, she doesn't mean that, of course she doesn't, she fought for her people, killed for her people, and she'd do it all again. But that doesn't mean she's psychotic. She killed because it was war, she killed because that was what she had to do. There was no pleasure in it, just a constant slog towards victory and freedom. She turns to him and smiles.

'Of course I mean it, just a shame I missed you, *Prince*.'

She turns back and carries on in the direction they were going. Ahead of her she sees a small sign on a street cutting off to their left.

'Swallow Avenue,' she says. 'Coming?'

She turns up the street and, for all her bravado, drops her pace to a slow walk. It's a residential street, lots of windows, lots of places someone could be lying in wait.

Charlie knows she's trying to get a reaction from him. Knowing it doesn't stop him wanting to lash out at her though. What is it about Quill that can play him so well, can get under his skin and really make him burn?

'There's no sign of him,' he says.

'No, did you really think there would be?'

They walk up the road a little way, obliviously passing the entrance to the courtyard on their left. From the end of the street they can hear the sound of music playing loudly from an upstairs window, someone singing very earnestly about love while thrashing seven shades out of an acoustic guitar. Further off there's the sound of children laughing, end of school, kids kicking out. A small motorbike suddenly farts its way past the end of the street making them both jump.

'So what now?' he asks. 'You want to start knocking door to door?'

'Oi!' someone shouts from behind them. 'If we'd known you were coming this way anyway we wouldn't have gone to the trouble.'

They both turn and, in the mouth of the road leading to the courtyard they see what looks like April, Tanya and Matteusz, but isn't. It was Tanya's voice speaking, and April's joins in.

'We couldn't believe it when Steve here told us where we were heading,' she says. 'We followed you all the way here. Unbelievable!' She laughs.

'I thought you were bound to spot us.' Tanya again. 'But you were too busy tearing chunks out of each other to notice us, weren't you?'

211

'Well,' says Quill, walking slowly towards them, a smile on her face, 'I've noticed you now.' She's feeling in a distinctly poisonous mood. She does hope somebody wants to make her do something energetic and fun.

Tanya suddenly grabs Matteusz, who until now has been standing awkwardly between them, clearly wishing he was anywhere but here. She holds the knife to his throat.

'Don't get excitable,' Tanya says. 'Slitting this kid's throat won't bother me. I've done worse. A *lot* worse in fact. I once spent an entire afternoon inserting knitting needles into an annoying pensioner, so please, threaten me. I'm happy to get the pavement dirty.'

'Please don't!' shouts Charlie and inwardly Quill curses. Never wear your heart on your sleeve in war, idiot, your enemy can cut it so easily.

'In public?' she asks, gesturing to the houses around. 'You really think that's a good idea?'

Tanya shrugs. 'What do I care? This isn't me, is it? I can do what I like. That's the whole bloody point, isn't it?'

Charlie walks past Quill. 'Just let him go,' he says. 'It's fine, honestly, we'll come with you.'

'Oh, will we?' Quill asks.

Charlie turns to her and, after all the anger, all the insults and fighting, the look on his face isn't one of belligerence, it's pure, naked pleading. 'Please,' he says. 'Please do as they say.'

She stares at the faces of April, Tanya and Matteusz a moment longer. Matteusz's contorted into a truly infant state of terror. Even though the life of the man occupying his body isn't really on the line, he looks like he's going to cry. 'These are not warriors,' she thinks. 'Let them have their little moment, and when their guard drops…'

'Fine,' she says, 'lead the way.'

27

GARRY FLETCHER NEEDS TO TURN OVER A NEW LEAF

Fletcher has spent the last half an hour flitting between utter confidence and an urge to fetch a large can of petrol and a box of matches. Stood in the locked room, staring at the stinking remains he's built his little empire on, he can't help but think he's made a few mistakes.

This place has only been six months of his life and yet it's already earned a fortune. It's a nightmare to run and the hours are excruciating (he takes a couple of days off a week, but the other five days can see him here from first thing in the morning to gone midnight). He doesn't plan on doing it forever. Not just because it's hard, but also because he knows that, sooner or later, something *will* go seriously wrong. If the machine were to break, he could never fix it (that's been proven today); if the aliens he appropriated it off returned they might take it off him; he deals with some very dangerous clients, what they get up to during transfers proves that, and one of them could decide to kill him. Or he could simply get caught by the law; he's not quite sure how but who knows? Only an idiot assumes he's invulnerable.

Yes, it's a shaky business. A business with a limited time frame. But he really can't have it fall apart yet because he's still not made anywhere near enough money. This hasn't exactly been a cheap start-up. He now owns this building. He's had the electrics fixed and a proper full-size back-up generator installed. He paid out a fair whack to Mike, though admittedly he nipped that expenditure in the bud after a few months. Now he pays Steve (and he's clearly not worth it but there you go). Basically he's been haemorrhaging cash from the beginning and is only just starting to build a decent profit. So the last thing he wants to do is kiss goodbye to all of it. But, if this is a sinking ship, he doesn't want to go down with it either.

He moves back to the transfer room, locking the door again on the remains of the aliens.

He starts experimenting with the machine, working the switches, exploring the functions. As always, that little voice is in his head helping to guide his fingers just a little (if you were going to design a machine that reads its operator's mind, why not go the whole bloody hog? If they had, he wouldn't be having any of these problems, it would know what he wanted to achieve and would just show him).

He needs to figure out how the cock-up today happened. He may have fixed it but what if it happens again? He needs to be able to work this thing properly. No more 'getting away with it' – it's too important.

'What went wrong with you?' he asks it, as if it might suddenly make life easier and talk back. He walks himself through the process.

'Map, yes,' he brings up the map, 'then scan.' He presses the button and the various lights showing viable transfers appear. 'There we go, lots of viable transfers. Choose your location, pick one…' he does, then follows the light around the surface of the pyramid to the next flat surface. 'And Bob? He would be your uncle,' he says, 'while Fanny is most definitely your aunt,' he stabs at the light. 'Transfer selected, channelled through to headset…' he moves around again where the operator chooses the headset. 'And boom…' he holds off on tapping the light one last time, not having anyone to transfer. He steps back, sighing.

'Simple, it's really, really simple... So what am I missing? How did that happen this morning? What else can this thing do that I'm just not seeing?'

Frustrated, he kicks at the base of the pyramid. 'Balls to you.'

This is getting him nowhere. He also needs to check the car. He hasn't had time to take a proper look at it. What if he's been driving around in a thing with bloodstains on the bumper?

He walks out of the transfer room and pauses in the doorway. The mess in the room at the end. Why has he been so slack about that? He ditched the kid as soon as possible, shoved him in the boot of his car and drove him miles away, burying him out in the country. But the aliens? They were just so... gruesome. It was a job he'd kept putting off. He figured that nobody could do him for it, it's not like they were human remains after all. So it felt like something he could let slide. In the beginning, he'd kept pushing Mike to help him clear it out but it never happened and then Mike... Well, Mike wasn't in a position to help him any more, was he? There was no way he was letting anybody else see in there and he hadn't fancied doing it on his own.

Slackness. That's basically all it was. He'd put it off and then it had become one of those invisible jobs, the sort you only remember need doing when you're in no position to actually do them. He'd been so busy with the day-to-day stuff that whole weeks would go by without him even thinking about it. But look at today, look at how being slack had nearly cost him everything.

He needs to take better care. A new start. He'll clear that room, get rid of useless Steve ... (actually wait, no, he'll make *Steve* clear the room, convince him it was penance for him screwing up, and *then* get rid of him – much better idea). He'll get these aliens to teach him a few tricks, then he'll get rid of them too. No loose ends.

Maybe he should be shot of Banks and Taylor too? Yes! Why not? Clean slate. Get this place sorted from top to bottom, proper organised and then make his money quickly and safely before setting fire to the lot and making a run for Dubai or somewhere.

O'Donnell's body. He'd just left that in the street. That was probably OK because there was nothing to link him to it, but still. Only an idiot leaves the evidence of his crimes in the middle of the road. Too late now, it'll be found – probably has been already – and it'll be written off as just another hit and run that would never get solved. You read about them in the paper all the time. Yes, he'll get away with that. Probably. Hopefully. Slack again though. Proper slack. He'd got angry and the anger had stopped him thinking straight. He's lucky he's got away with all this as long as he has: time to sort himself out.

He goes outside to look at the car. It actually isn't too bad. A major dent on the bonnet where O'Donnell impacted but there's no blood. He'd flipped right over and hit the road behind. 'What about when you reversed over him?' he thinks. So he moves round to the rear and scoots down to examine the back wheel. There's sign of trouble here alright, but you'd have to be looking for it. The inside of the wheel arches are splattered with blood and there's some skin and hair in the tyre treads. Good going over with a pressure hose and that would be dealt with. Do that and then he'll just get shot of it. He knows a few people in the motor trade. As long as there's nothing incriminating on the thing he'll happily let it go for a song, no questions asked. But he'll do it today, as soon as he can, as soon as this business with the aliens is sorted, because he has to stop letting things slide.

Good, yes, this feels good. This feels like an important new start.

He checks his watch. What's keeping them? Maybe he should have gone himself after all? Passing something like this off onto others, that maybe wasn't such a good idea. Something else to bear in mind for the future.

He stands up and he must have done it too quickly because all of a sudden his head is swimming. See? This is what happens when you don't look after things, he thinks, his vision blurring. Garry Fletcher, you need to turn over a new leaf.

28

IT IS NOW

Quill and Charlie lead the way into the courtyard, Charlie constantly looking over his shoulder to keep an eye on Matteusz. He's lost so many people he cares about. In fact, up until a few weeks ago he would have said he had lost all of them. But life doesn't work like that, does it? Just when you think you have nothing left to lose you stumble on something new to cling to, desperate, terrified, after a life whose main lesson seems to have been to prove the fragility of others.

'Stop it,' whispers Quill. 'You're only making it easier for them.'

'What does it matter? They've got what they want.'

She shakes her head. 'We don't know *what* they want yet, so stop telling them how they'll be able to get it.'

He can see the sense in this but it's hard, he has no idea how she can remain so numb, so removed from everything. For all their arguments, he knows there's another Quill inside the one she shows, another Quill she'll never let him know.

'Building on the left,' says Tanya. 'Get inside and stop muttering to each other, play any tricks and I'll get cutting.'

Quill opens the door to Fletcher's building and pushes past Charlie so that she enters first. It's an automatic gesture but he spots it all the same; she's putting herself in the line of fire, defending him.

The rest follow and Steve shouts out in Matteusz's voice, 'Sir? Mr Fletcher? It's me, Steve. We've got them!'

Steve looks at the two girls either side of him, seeing them as Banks and Taylor and impatient to get out of their grip and back in a position of relative safety.

'That's enough now,' he says to them. 'We're here, we've got them, and if you remember, I happen to work here.'

Tanya laughs. 'I wouldn't employ you.'

'Let him go Banksy,' says April, 'he's got a point.'

Tanya shrugs. 'Fine.'

Charlie visibly relaxes as Steve walks past reception in the body of the boy he'd really like to keep alive.

'Sir?' Steve calls again.

Fletcher appears from the transfer room. For a moment he appears almost surprised to see them. 'Alright, alright, calm down, I'm here.' He sees the rest of them. 'And you've been busy I see?'

Tanya steps forward. 'Told you we'd get them, didn't we?'

'Walk in the park,' April agrees, 'though I wouldn't mind swapping back now if you don't mind. Day's getting on and this isn't quite what I had in mind for my session, you know? I want to get myself inside someone comfortable!'

'Yeah,' says Tanya, 'time for some real partying.'

Fletcher appears to eye them up for a minute and then nods. 'Of course.' He looks at Steve. 'Do you want to do the honours?'

Charlie still can't quite process how strange it is to see a face he knows so well move in so unfamiliar a way. Steve is shocked to be asked to operate the machine.

'Me?' he asks.

'You can manage can't you?' Fletcher asks. 'Or do you need me to hold your hand?'

Tanya laughs at this. 'He's got your number!' she says. 'You should have seen him out there,' she continues, and this is enough to get Steve moving; the last thing he wants is for Banks or Taylor to start telling Fletcher how useless he is.

'Of course I can manage,' he says, interrupting. 'Come on then,' he says to Tanya and April, 'let's get you changed back.'

They walk past him and into the transfer room.

'Not just changed back,' says Tanya, 'relocated! I've an evening of fun ahead of me!'

'Yeah, yeah,' Steve replies.

'Good lad,' says Fletcher. 'And while you're doing that, I'll talk to our new friends.'

Steve nods and follows Tanya and April into the transfer room. 'Just give me a sec,' he says, moving over to the machine. He hopes Fletcher knows what he's doing, once he's reversed these three transfers and sent Banks and Taylor onto God knows where they want to be, he and his boss are going to be outnumbered in here. It'll be five on two if they decide they're going to kick off. Steve's not entirely sure he cares. As far as he's concerned, today's taught him something: his neck is on the line and what good is money if you're too dead to spend it? He's no idea if Fletcher will let him stop working here – probably not, he knows too much – but he's put some of his wages aside. He could just do a bunk with it, take the wife and kids and maybe head north, Manchester or Leeds. He used to have a girlfriend who came from Leeds, it wasn't a bad place. He'd keep his head down and make a fresh go of things. Maybe he'd finally be able to get over the drink, too (though even thinking about it makes him thirsty for oblivion).

'So where do you want to go?' he asks the other two.

'I'm not bothered,' says Tanya. 'I'll make my own fun when I get there!'

'Yeah,' April agrees, 'roll of the dice, like it! Just send us off and we'll get the party started.'

'Fine.' God these two really are a pair of immature pricks. He wishes he knew how to get the machine to tell him the age of the viable transfers: he'd love nothing more than to dump them into the bodies of a pair of babies for the evening. They could sit there crying and filling their nappies.

'What are you smiling at?' Tanya asks.

'Nothing,' says Steve and presses the buttons that will reverse the transfers. April and Tanya both look dizzy and stumble slightly. Steve immediately transfers Banks and Taylor back out.

Tanya looks at him. 'Matteusz?' What just happened?'

Steve works quickly to reverse his own transfer. He doesn't want to get stuck in a conversation with whoever these two really are, let the boss handle it.

He presses the light that stands for Matteusz and then, for one happy moment, all goes black as he momentarily hangs between bodies.

Then it's light again and he's lying on the bench, head swimming. It's always so disorientating coming back from a transfer. It's like coming out of a drink binge but without the blessed drink. He rubs his face, closing his eyes, willing the headache to calm down.

Slowly, carefully, he sits up, takes his headset off and takes a few deep breaths. He needs to get it together quick, in case those kids try and cause any trouble.

'Rise and shine,' Fletcher says and already Steve is feeling that sinking dread that he's grown to feel whenever his boss looks at him.

'All done,' he says. 'Just feeling a bit woozy.'

He looks up and sees Fletcher staring at him. It looks wrong though because the others, the woman and the four kids, they're stood either side of him. They don't look like prisoners, they look sort of like, well… friends.

'Sir?' he asks. 'Is everything alright?'

'It is now,' says Fletcher and punches him square in the middle of his blinding headache.

29

NO MORE TIME AT ALL

A short while ago:

O'Donnell hangs up on Fletcher and looks at the house he's followed the aliens to. Can he trust Fletcher? He doubts that, doubts it very much in fact. Perhaps, though, he does owe him a chance to state his case. O'Donnell can hardly claim the moral high ground, not after the things he's done. Fletcher wants a chance to walk away from all this without risking exposure to the authorities; O'Donnell supposes he can't blame him.

He imagines the consequences of this all being over. Making the decision not to keep this body now was one thing, accepting he might be stuck with the flabby reality of his own body *forever*, that's something else entirely.

He starts walking. He doubts the aliens are going anywhere, and even if they do, this is obviously where they live: didn't one of them take a set of keys from its pocket and open the door? Fletcher has said he'll be twenty minutes so why waste those minutes just standing on a street corner? He wants to make the most of his time, even if that's just by walking for a while, feeling how easy that is in this young body.

He breaks into a jog, because he can. If he tried this in his real body he'd be breathless and hurting already, that big belly of his shaking and straining with every step. He really should look after himself more, he supposes, there just never seemed much point. Ugly on the inside, ugly on the outside, why pretend to be anything else?

The jog turns into a run, the run turns into a sprint, and by now he's on Great Eastern Street and people are staring because he's actually laughing out loud. If this is his last moment of freedom, he's going to really *feel* it.

He runs from his life. He runs from his mind. He runs from his mother. He runs until he can't ever imagine being still again.

Then, all of a sudden, it feels as if something's hit him, a colossal weight that threatens to send him toppling to the floor.

The view has changed, he's no longer where he was. How's that possible? He looks down at his own body, suddenly, horribly, condensed around him again and feels the urge to scream. Not now! Not yet! He wanted more time, a few minutes, just a little more...

He turns around just in time to see the car bearing down on him, the snarling face of Fletcher behind the wheel.

And then John O'Donnell has no more time at all.

30

PICKING UP THE BASICS

Ram had been running, running for his life from that bastard in the car. His borrowed body fighting him every step of the way, pulling, straining, wheezing, crying out, and then... he's himself again, running down Great Eastern Street with absolutely no idea what's just happened.

He stops running, looks around, feels his own body returned to him and, if people hadn't been staring before, they certainly do now as he laughs and cheers and starts leaping up and down right there in the middle of the pavement.

'Must be on something,' a woman mutters as she walks past, giving him a wide berth.

'High on being me, beautiful!' he says, blowing her a kiss. She acts as if it might be toxic, flinching as if it hits her, and scampers away at speed.

He has no idea how this has just happened but couldn't care less. He's back.

But could they change him again? With the flick of a switch he might find himself trapped in another body. No. Ram's not having that happen, not if he can help it. These people need sorting. Hopefully Tanya is bringing help, he needs to get back over there as quickly as he can.

He starts running again, cutting through Leonard Street, aiming to get back to Swallow Avenue as fast as possible.

When he arrives, he looks around but there's no sign of anyone, maybe they've found the office? Or maybe Fletcher has tricked them somehow? He hovers in indecision, he should probably wait and see but Ram isn't in the mood for wait and see. He rarely is.

Moving carefully, he enters the courtyard and creeps over to Fletcher's building. He peers through the door: no sign of anyone. He takes a deep breath and tries the door: it's open.

He steps inside and moves through reception, bracing himself to run at the first sign of trouble. The place is silent, could it be empty? Have they all cleared off? Maybe that's why he was swapped back? Maybe they just turned everything off and are now on the run?

He reaches the transfer room and peeks inside. He can see three people lying on the benches: two strangers and Eighties Rock. So where's the boss?

Suddenly he hears the sound of a door opening further down the corridor. If he steps out of the transfer room he'll be seen. Does he mind that? Is he happy to take Fletcher on? Part of him certainly is, another part of him wonders whether it would be better to hang back, see what's going on and *then* act. Tanya and the rest of them aren't here (or are they now locked in that little room like he was?).

Feet are approaching along the corridor. He makes a decision. When he first woke up he was frustrated by how dark this room was, now it's a blessing as he rolls under one of the benches.

Fletcher walks into the room, glances at the three men already connected to the machine and then starts tinkering with it.

'What went wrong with you?' he says and Ram half expects the machine to answer him back. It doesn't, but Ram watches closely as Fletcher starts working his way through the controls.

'Map, yes…' Fletcher says, and Ram can just about see a stylised map of the area appear on the screen. 'Then scan,' Fletcher continues, pressing a button. At this point the map fills with little points of light.

'There we go,' says Fletcher, 'lots of viable transfers. Choose your location…' Ram can see him scrolling across the map as if it were a touch screen: zooming in, scanning left and right. 'Pick one…' Fletcher taps on one of the lights. Ram watches as the light swells and then appears to zip round to the next panel.

'And Bob? He would be your uncle,' Fletcher says, 'while Fanny is most definitely your aunt.'

It's harder for Ram to see now but Fletcher clearly taps on the light.

'Transfer selected,' he says, 'Channelled through to headset…'

Fletcher moves around again and once more taps the panel. 'And boom…'

He goes to tap one last time but holds off. He steps back and sighs.

'Simple, it's really, really simple, so what am I missing? How did that happen this morning? What else can this thing do that I'm just not seeing?'

He kicks at the base of the pyramid. 'Balls to you.'

Ram wonders whether he can surprise Fletcher, but from his position under the bench it would take too long to crawl out and get to his feet. It doesn't matter anyway as Fletcher suddenly walks out of the room.

Ram gets out from his hiding place and moves to the doorway. He can hear Fletcher going outside. Maybe he could lock the man out? Threaten to destroy the machine? No, who knows when the other three might wake up? He'd soon be outnumbered then.

Then he has an idea. He almost dismisses it; he's just got his body back after all, does he really want to risk losing it again? Still, if he pulls this off he'll be able to do whatever he wants. He'll be the boss!

He moves over to the machine and retraces the steps he's just watched Fletcher go through. He needs to be quick: Fletcher could come back any minute.

He brings up the map, finds this building on it, then zooms right in. He can see one light inside – that must be me, the others aren't… what was the word Fletcher used? *Viable*. Yes, the others aren't viable because they're already connected.

Right outside the building there's another light. That has to be Fletcher. He taps it. The light moves around to the next panel. This is where Ram couldn't see quite so clearly but interestingly there's a tingle in his head, a sense that the machine is trying to help him. There's a strange collection of letters next to the light now; they mean nothing to Ram and yet somehow, thanks to that tingling, he knows they mean 'confirm'. He taps them. The light swells and moves to the next panel.

Now Ram can see ten different icons, three of which are blue, the rest are red. The headsets he thinks, this is how you choose which headset. The three in blue are the three already in use. So I need to pick one and... he holds off from tapping it, he needs to be wearing the headset, doesn't he?

He looks around, grabs the closest one, puts it on and then matches where the cable connects on the machine with the diagram in front of him.

If he wasn't panicking about Fletcher returning, this is the point where he might still have backed out, but he's rushing, he's desperate to get this done before he hears the front door open again. He taps the icon for the headset he's wearing and a warm dizziness settles through his head. Is this it? Is it working? He glances at the screen to see that strange collection of writing again, the same as he saw on the other panel. Of course, Fletcher was about to tap one last time, his finger had hovered over the screen. Ram taps on the graphic he somehow knows means 'confirm' and then his body falls to the floor, empty.

But Ram doesn't know that because he's leaning back against Fletcher's car having taken possession of the man himself.

'Freaky,' he mutters, rubbing his face.

It's nowhere near as disorientating as when he woke up in O'Donnell's body. This is just a simple transfer. Aside from a few seconds' imbalance as he adapts to moving in Fletcher's body, Ram is firing on all four cylinders by the time he's back in the transfer room. He needs to hide his body.

It's really weird looking down at himself, lying on the floor, face slack, arms and legs splayed. You only ever see yourself in a mirror and he realises it's just not the same. Picking himself up is even stranger, feeling what he feels like to other people. Just so, so weird.

He does it carefully, worried that he might somehow break the connection. He cradles his head and keeps an eye on the wire to ensure the headset doesn't come off. He pulls his body over to the bench he hid under before stashing himself in the same place.

Then he moves back along the wire, tucking it out of the way so it's not too obvious and not so taut that someone might catch it and disconnect it.

All done. He thinks he just might get away with this.

He hears the front door swing open, and is hit by a sudden wave of nerves. He really hopes nobody asks him anything he can't bluff.

'Sir?' he hears someone shout and the voice seems familiar and yet, somehow, *not,* all at the same time. 'Mr Fletcher? It's me, Steve. We've got them!'

Steve? Who's Steve? And *who* has he got?

This is already threatening to be more than he can handle. He shakes himself out of his panic; he's the boss here, remember? He can just brazen it out. If somebody doesn't like it, he'll just shout at them until they accept it.

'Sir?' The voice calls again.

Ram takes a deep breath and steps out of the transfer room. He finds himself face-to-face with Matteusz. That's why the voice was familiar, it was just lacking an accent.

Beyond Matteusz he can see Quill and Charlie, clearly hostages, with April and Tanya behind. Except it's not April or Tanya, is it? He can tell by the way they're walking, swaggering really, down the corridor towards him.

The three people on the benches, the two men and Eighties Rock, this is them. They've taken over the bodies of his friends.

He realises he hasn't said anything.

'Alright, alright, calm down, I'm here,' he says, nodding towards Quill and Charlie. 'And you've been busy, I see?'

Tanya steps forward. 'Told you we'd get them, didn't we?'

'Walk in the park,' adds April, 'though I wouldn't mind swapping back now if you don't mind. Day's getting on and this isn't quite what I had in mind for my session, you know? I want to get myself inside someone comfortable!'

'Yeah,' Tanya agrees, 'time for some real partying.'

OK, so Tanya and April must be the two guys he hasn't met before. Clients by the sound of it. Which means Matteusz is really Eighties Rock. Fine. He's up to speed. The sooner Tanya and April are back to normal and these two are transferred somewhere else, the better for all concerned.

He's pulled it off once but he really doesn't want to try operating the machine in front of other people. If they see how uncertain he is, it might give the game away. Best to let Eighties Rock do it.

'Of course,' he says, looking at Matteusz. 'Do you want to do the honours?'

Matteusz looks shocked. 'Me?' he asks.

Has he blown this? Surely Eighties Rock must know how to use the thing if he works here?

'You can manage, can't you?' he asks, because what choice does he have except to brave this out? 'Or do you need me to hold your hand?'

Whoever it is that has taken over Tanya laughs at this. 'He's got your number!' she says. 'You should have seen him out there,' she adds, and this seems to make Eighties Rock panic.

'Of course I can manage,' he says, all flustered. 'Come on then,' he says beckoning to Tanya and April, 'let's get you changed back.'

All three of them head past Ram and into the transfer room.

'Not just changed back,' Tanya says as she passes, 'relocated! I've an evening of fun ahead of me!'

'Yeah, yeah,' replies Eighties Rock.

'Good lad,' says Ram, looking at Quill and Charlie. 'And while you're doing that, I'll talk to our new friends.'

He hastily gestures for the two of them to back up down the corridor. They ignore him. In fact, Quill raises an eyebrow and looks as if she's about to say something. Panicking, Ram puts his fingers to his lips and desperately mimes for her to be quiet. She's so surprised that she doesn't say a word.

He leans in close, flinching as she clenches her fists, ready to punch him.

'It's me!' he whispers. 'Ram! Now move back into the reception, quick!'

She narrows her eyes, but he can see that Charlie believes him because he smiles and moves back down the corridor. After a second, Quill follows and the three of them turn around the corner where they can speak more freely.

'I swapped with the bloke running this place,' Ram explains. 'You know they can do that, yeah?'

'No,' says Quill. 'We just assumed that April, Tanya and Matteusz all chose the same day to enjoy a nervous breakdown.'

Ram rolls his eyes at her sarcasm.

'You know how to work the machine then?' Charlie asks.

Ram shrugs. 'I'm not stupid, I picked up the basics.' This is overselling things rather but he likes being the clever one for once. 'When Eighties Rock back there swaps everyone over—'

'Eighties Rock?' Charlie asks.

'The one that looks like Matteusz,' Ram says. 'He works here.'

'Weird name.'

'Just shut up for a minute, will you?' Ram can't believe this kid sometimes. 'When he's changed the other three back, he's going to transfer the two blokes straight out again. Which means they're not a problem, they'll just be lying there sparked out.'

'So we only have one person to deal with?' asks Quill. 'This "Eighties Rock" of yours.'

'Yeah. I think his name might actually be Steve, now I think about it but, yeah, there'll just be him.'

'What a pity,' Quill sighs. 'I was looking forward to more of a fight than that. Oh well, I suppose one's better than nothing.'

'Not a chance,' says Ram, as they walk back towards the transfer room, 'he's mine.'

In the transfer room, April, Tanya and Matteusz are looking confused but Charlie holds his fingers to his lips and leads them over to where Steve is waking up.

'Rise and shine,' says Ram.

'All done,' Steve says, 'just feeling a bit woozy.'

Steve looks towards them and, just for one beautiful moment, Ram soaks up the look of worry on the man's face.

'Sir?' Steve asks. 'Is everything alright?'

'It is now,' Ram says and breaks his nose.

31

STEVE NEGOTIATES FOR THE CONTINUED USE OF HIS LEGS

Steve's lap is full of blood. He just knew today was going down the drain.

'Let me explain to you what's about to happen,' says Quill, and he looks up at her and fights the urge to cry. He can tell that this is not someone who will be swayed by the sight of a few tears.

'The happy children are away being happy,' she continues, 'doing the hugging and backslapping that they so love to do. They will be swapping stories, bringing each other up to speed. You know, the boring stuff.'

'He hit me,' says Steve, 'Fletcher hit me.'

'Do use a brain cell, Steve of the Eighties Rock. That wasn't your boss, that was one of my lot. He took over the body of your boss so as to indulge in all the turning of tables and punching of noses.'

'Oh.'

'Concisely put. So, as I was saying, we have reached the stage of your day where all the pain starts to happen.'

'What?' Steve tries backing away but that's nigh-on impossible when you're sat on a bench, so really he just ends up scrunching himself into a ball like a hedgehog. A hedgehog with a broken nose.

'Why?' he asks.

'Why?' Quill sits down on the end of the bench and smiles at him. He's not sure, because his panic is making his nerves get all confused, but he thinks that smile may have just caused his bladder to empty.

'Well,' she continues, 'let's see. Maybe it's because you've been part of a business that has been using alien technology to offer body tourism? Letting the rich occupy the bodies of others,' she leans in, 'without, of course, their explicit approval, a point that particularly sets my knuckles whitening.' She sniffs something unpleasant and leans back. He guesses he must have wet himself after all.

'As if that act of violation wasn't enough,' she continues, 'these rich body tourists have then been going around committing acts of violence and murder, spreading the misery far and wide.' She sighs. 'Stealing people's lives wasn't sufficient, you had to end the lives of those close to them too.'

'I don't know anything about that,' he says. 'Fletcher gave clients free rein, no questions asked. I just worked here. Keeping an eye on things, a bit of tidying ...'

'A bit of kidnapping?'

'What?' He realises she means what he, Banks and Taylor have just done. 'Oh, that, well Fletcher insisted, I thought he was going to kill me. I just didn't know!'

'Well,' says Quill, 'let me remove any similar doubt from your current position. I won't kill you.'

'No?' Steve looks relieved.

'No, I'm afraid not. Sorry. I know you'll want me to after the torture really gets into full swing but, I have principles, not many, but I draw the line at murder. I may handicap you for life, reduce you to a paralysed, vegetative state ...' she laughs. 'It's always so hard to predict when you get carried away. Human bodies are so fragile, one cut here and that's your spinal cord gone, one stab there and you're vacating into a bag for the rest of your life.'

'Oh God!' Now Steve does start crying, sobbing and sobbing. He hasn't cried this much since he could count his birthdays on one hand. 'Please don't hurt me, I'll do whatever you want but don't hurt me!'

Quill sucks air in between her teeth, as if caught on the thorns of a particularly tough decision. 'I'm not sure I can trust you. Well, obviously I can't, no, sorry, I think it has to be the torture.'

'But I'll tell you everything I know! All of his clients, he keeps them in a notebook in his pocket. The room at the end of the corridor, there's something awful in there that he never lets me see.' He has a sudden brainwave: 'The machine! I can work it better than he can! I figured out how to do a full swap, two people completely transferred!' He doesn't admit this was an accident. 'And I figured out how to reverse that. He didn't have a clue. I did it while he was out… Awkward, actually because I think that means he probably killed Mr O'Donnell when he thought he was killing—'

Quill interrupts him. 'You're waffling.'

'But it means I can show you how it works, you could do whatever you want to do with it.'

Quill makes a show of considering again.

'OK, let's discuss this a little more. Maybe, just *maybe* I can leave you with the continued use of your legs after all.'

32

AN UNEXPECTEDLY BUSY
DAY FOR THE METROPOLITAN POLICE
SERVICE

Viola Cummings is not normally one for public displays. She simply hasn't got the confidence for it. Those that know her are, therefore, extremely surprised to hear the news that she has been arrested for running naked through the Barbican Centre.

If it were simply a matter of her public exposure, the sentence would have been relatively innocuous. But after a brief lap of the reception area, she then stole a backpack from a distracted tourist, strapped it on and gave local security the exercise workout of their lives while screaming, 'Bomb! I have a bomb! Going to blow this whole place sky high!'

This behaviour resulted in a more severe sentence.

Initially, a weeping Ms Cummings spent a considerable amount of time as an unwilling guest of the security services (constantly insisting she had no idea what anyone was talking about; not only would she not expose herself within the Barbican centre, she'd never owned a backpack in her life). She was then forced to serve a lengthy term of community service plus compulsory counselling sessions.

The latter actually proved useful and she would later admit (to her entirely new set of friends, it's funny what being on a terrorism watchlist does for your social circle) counselling had been the making of her.

James Banks, property developer and terrible human being, also has a bad day.

It's extremely confusing. One minute he'd been preparing to start a fight in a particularly rough pub, happily ensconced inside the body of an eighteen-year-old from Brixton. The next thing he knows he's himself again and being thrown out of the back seat of a car. He doesn't hurt himself much in the fall, though he does get a sudden glimpse of the driver, the blonde woman he and Taylor were sent to kidnap earlier. How's this happening? Has Fletcher tried to shaft him or something?

Then, for a period of five minutes, he knows nothing at all. The policeman currently standing next to his hospital bed assures him that he ran into a pound shop and started punching the goods. When the store manager tried to restrain him, he ran out into the road and attempted to karate kick an approaching minivan. The manoeuvre did not work out well for him, as the heroic quantity of plaster and bandages now covering his body attest.

The unusual experiences of Barry Taylor, financial analyst and self-proclaimed 'bit of a lad' are, initially, not dissimilar. He too, experienced a brief moment of being pulled out of one encounter and into another.

He had been weighing up his options between a pretty brunette and a pretty blonde, half tempted to take on both.

Then, he'd found himself briefly awake, the blonde woman he'd followed earlier grinning down at him.

After that, the next thing he knows he's squatting in the open doorway of his boss's office at work.

Later, he will have the impossible task of trying to explain a considerable quantity of illegal pornographic material on his work computer's hard drive. But that, and the court trial it will lead to are all future problems. Right now he is staring his boss in the eye and wondering quite how he's going to laugh off the fact that he's pleasuring himself with a gold-plated industry award.

The conversation does not go well.

* * *

To begin with, the police aren't sure what to do with Imogen Farmer. She's walked in off the street with a story they simply can't believe. She claims that she's the one responsible for the fire at the Collins' household. That it's down to her that Max Collins, still tearfully insisting his innocence, has been charged with the murder of his family.

The evidence against the boy is so clear that they simply can't accept the crime could be attributed to someone else, as much as they might wish otherwise.

While Ms Farmer seems clearly frustrated at not being believed, she can't actually give them any reason to change their mind. Eventually, the police officer in charge of the case insists she be taken away and charged for wasting their time. At which point, Ms Farmer goes through a period of extreme disorientation. The court will later hear – indeed it will form part of the evidence for 'diminished responsibility' – that she looked around and asked what she was doing there.

When, with more patience than she truly feels, the lead officer explains the events of the last hour or so, Ms Farmer breaks down in tears. She then begins to give far more useful evidence. She describes the precise method she used for starting the fire; the removal of the battery from the fire alarm ('I put it in his pocket,' she says); the places where she poured the petrol; even young Tommy's pyjamas and the plastic ties she used to fix him to the chair.

The police are at a loss as to explain how it's possible but a court later decides that they'd much rather convict a woman who has all the conviction of committing the crime than a child who doesn't. Max Collins will be in care for the next few years, but at least he won't be in prison.

There are many similar cases. All involving affluent individuals, all involving bizarre lapses in behaviour, acts of public self-sabotage, police confessions... It is a strange day indeed for the Metropolitan Police Service.

And finally, there is the curious case of Mr Garry Fletcher.

It isn't the first time the police have had someone confess to a hit and run. It's actually surprisingly common. Guilt has a habit of building over time, and he won't be the first motorist to suddenly realise he has to atone for what he's done.

Yes, it is strange that he will change his opinion so completely, shortly after having submitted his signed statement. His screaming and the violent manner he hurls himself around his cell is put down to a psychological breakdown. No doubt this is also why he now insists: 'I didn't say any of that! It wasn't me! It was the aliens!'

On the subject of aliens, what really surprises the investigating officer is the mess he finds in the back seat of Fletcher's car. Almost every available space is filled with what appears – but simply can't be – body parts. Legs, arms, torsos, but all of a strange, clearly non-human variety. Sitting amongst all this, and the one claiming it to be of extra-terrestrial origin, is a man who is alternatively sobbing and vomiting. The man is identified as Steve Hopley and he later admits to being complicit in the hit and run.

The investigating officer is inclined to view the body parts as some form of strange hoax – though they will later be removed from evidence by a team from UNIT, so who knows what the real story is?

Regardless of the sundry limbs and organs, Fletcher's car offers clear evidence tying it to the hit and run of one John O'Donnell, a businessman whose wife will later appear on the news, weeping and offering words of adulation in the memory of her 'kind and loyal husband'.

Fletcher's statement, effectively a signed confession, is the icing on the cake.

With that, the case against Mr Fletcher and his accomplice would seem closed. If not for the fact that the forensic team also find trace evidence in the boot of the car linking it to the disappearance of a young boy from the area.

Garth Todd, ten years old, had gone missing six months earlier and, despite some confusing witness statements that claimed to have seen him wandering the streets in the company of an adult late on the night of his disappearance, the investigation had floundered. There was no evidence to link the family with his disappearance and, while the papers had run with the story, in the ghoulish way papers will do, it had been generally accepted by law-enforcement officials that the case would remain unsolved.

This new evidence, clearly placing the boy's body in the boot of Fletcher's car, opens new avenues for investigation. When pressed for an explanation, Fletcher, by all accounts a broken man, finally admits to burying the body and gives vague directions that allow it to be found.

Even at his trial he insists he didn't murder young Garth. Indeed, he trots out the by now familiar claim that it was all the fault of aliens.

Obviously, nobody believes him.

33

SAY NOTHING

They attend Poppy's funeral, surrounded by ghoulish press, all hoping for a human-interest piece about the girl who drove a stolen car through a shop window. Quill is the only obvious absence. She sees 'nothing worthwhile in immersing herself in weird human rituals'.

Ram's father had tried to come too. Ram knew it was less about showing his support and more about being terrified to let his son out of his sight, so he'd vetoed it.

Ram feels sorry for the panic he's put his dad through but he's not about to explain what happened, that wouldn't set his mind at rest. He's maintained the fiction of having needed some space and has played the same card now, to ensure he can turn up without a parent in tow.

April and Tanya accompany him on either side, with Charlie and Matteusz bringing up the rear.

They listen to the slow, confused sermon of a man who doesn't know what to say. They watch the red, crying faces of the family who don't know what to think.

And they say nothing, because there's nothing useful to say.

34
NORMAL

Ram finds April sat staring out at the playing field. The moment he spots her is awkward; she's obviously sitting there because she wants to be alone. He's walking there for exactly the same reason. So does he turn around and look rude by walking off? No, of course he doesn't, he decides he has no choice but to ruin both their plans by sitting next to her. Neither of them say anything for a bit, just a grunt of greeting and then a slightly awkward silence broken by the sound of Ram tearing up grass with his fingers.

'Are you OK?' April asks finally. Ram would normally get angry at the question but he knows she's asking because she doesn't know what else to say.

'Yeah,' he says. 'I spent a while thinking about what that old fat guy might have got up to and then gave up. I mean, it doesn't matter does it really?'

'No?'

'Not like I'll ever know. I'll never remember either. Wasn't me so there's no point in feeling guilty.' He shrugs and April can't help but wonder if he means a word of this. 'I guess I just realised I was beating myself up over something I couldn't control. What's the point?'

'I don't like not being in control.'

'Who does? Done now though. Yesterday's problem. There'll be something else to worry about soon enough, won't there?'

She gives a half smile. 'Probably.'

There's another moment of silence. Then Ram breaks it again. He thought he wanted silence but now he has it he realises it's just as stressful as noise.

'Do you miss being normal?' he asks. 'Because that's what really bothers me at the moment. All of this stuff that goes on now, stuff we haven't asked for. I mean, I'm not saying I wouldn't help people who needed it, of course I would, but it's like we've lost our own lives. All the plans, all the things we knew...' He stares up at the sky. 'I don't feel like I know anything any more.'

'Normal?' April shrugs. 'I don't know if I've ever been normal. I know what you mean but things are always changing aren't they? Things you thought were one thing turn out to be another, life keeps changing, building, U-turning. People are…'

'Annoying?'

She laughs. 'I was going to say surprising.'

'Surprising and annoying.'

'Some of them.'

Ram nods. 'I just want normal. Instead I have an alien leg and people trying to kill me three times a week.'

'And I have half an alien heart and a hangover during lunch break,' April sighs. 'You know what I think?'

'What?'

'I think this is the new normal and there's only one thing we can do about it.'

'What's that?'

'Get on with it.'

Ram nods. 'You're probably right.'

He gets up and brushes the loose blades of grass from the legs of his jeans.

'You off?' April asks.

'Yeah,' he says, 'guess I have some new normal to be getting on with.'

April watches him walk off to do just that.